Life or Death

Little
Sec

EMILY BLAKE

Life or Death

Point

No part of this publication may be reproduced, stored in a retrieval system, or transmitted in any form or by any means, electronic, mechanical, photocopying, recording, or otherwise, without written permission of the publisher. For information regarding permission, write to Scholastic Inc., Attention: Permissions Department, 557 Broadway, New York, NY 10012.

ISBN-13: 978-0-439-86720-7
ISBN-10: 0-439-86720-7

Copyright © 2008 by Scholastic Inc.

The text type was set in Utopia.
Book design by Steve Scott.

12 11 10 9 8 7 6 5 4 3 2 1   8 9 10 11 12 13/0

Printed in the U.S.A.   40

First printing May 2008

For Morgan,
who helped me pull through.

Life or Death

Little
Secrets

Chapter One

Zoey Ramirez stared unblinking at the ambulance racing ahead of her and said a silent prayer
that the girl inside it was alive. If anyone had
told Zoey two hours ago that she would care *at
all* if Audra Wilson lived or died, she would have
thought they were nuts. Two hours ago she had
no idea *this* was going to happen.

Squeezing her eyes shut, Zoey tried to block
out the lights and sirens flashing and screaming
around her, the metal grate between her and
the two police officers in the front seat, and the
realization that this was usually a seat for crimi-
nals. The wailing siren on the roof of the car
made her head ache. In the darkness behind

her eyelids, images flickered — a horror movie, the one she was living.

Zoey cringed at the scenes playing over and over in her mind. The argument on the bridge. The crazy look in Audra's eyes. Audra lunging at her. The chilling realization that her life was in real danger — and the quick step to the side that had sent Audra plummeting over the edge. Again, Zoey heard Audra's crazy laugh. Again, she felt her hand closing on air, and saw Audra's body slip beneath the white water. It had all happened so fast. It just didn't seem real.

After the fall, Zoey had felt like she was on autopilot. Clutching her useless cell phone, she'd started running. She ran until the tiny screen finally registered a signal, then dialed 911. Everything after that had been a blur of questions and sirens and adrenaline. She was still in that blur.

Zoey opened her eyes as the police car pulled up beside the ambulance at the emergency-room entrance of Silver Spring General Hospital. The driver turned off the sirens but left the lights flashing. Zoey craned her neck to see what was happening. She reached for the handle of the door, but found there was none. She was trapped in the police car, trapped in a nightmare. Pressing her forehead against the cold glass, Zoey watched as several medics rushed out of the emergency entrance toward the opening doors of the ambulance. They shivered in their scrubs, wrapping their arms around themselves to keep warm in the sharp autumn air. In some far-off spot in her mind, Zoey realized she was shivering, too, from shock and fear.

Zoey watched as the EMTs unloaded a metal gurney from the ambulance — the gurney bearing Audra's body. Catching a glimpse of Audra's dark, wet hair, Zoey's stomach twisted again. This was not some movie she was watching or some dream she would wake up from soon. This was real. Zoey looked away as the medics rushed the gurney inside, shouting to one another in hospital code.

The officer in the driver's seat got out and opened Zoey's door. "Let's go," he barked. Zoey felt like a criminal. If only she hadn't gotten into Audra's car. If only she'd caught Audra's hand. If only . . .

Feeling as though she was moving through

molasses, Zoey followed the cops into the ER. One of them pointed at a plastic seat in the corner. "Sit down and stay out of the way," he said, shoving Zoey toward the chair. "And don't go anywhere — we'll need to ask you some more questions." Zoey sank numbly into the seat and tried to process what was happening.

Several doctors rushed into the curtained area where they'd put Audra. In the gap of the fabric Zoey saw a blur of arms and tubes and machines. Someone was yelling orders. Nurses' shoes squeaked as they moved quickly across the tile floor. From inside the curtains, a machine beeped insistently. Surely the doctors wouldn't be in such a rush if Audra was already . . .

"Call it," a doctor said.

"Time of death: three-thirteen P.M.," another voice said loudly.

Oh no, oh no, oh no, Zoey repeated in her head. *Oh no, oh —*

"What's your name, kid?" The police officers were back, standing over her. The one who'd asked the question looked down at Zoey sternly, while the other officer scribbled notes on a small pad.

"Zoey Ramirez," Zoey said flatly.

"And the other girl?"

"Audra Wilson."

"Yeah, that's right. Why'd she jump?" the officer asked.

"She didn't," Zoey answered softly. She felt like she was watching herself from somewhere far away. Was this really happening? "She fell."

"Did you push her?" the officer said.

"What?" Zoey looked up, meeting his eyes. Was he kidding? The officer stared back evenly.

"Your friend. The dead girl. Did . . . you . . . push . . . her?" he asked again slowly, like Zoey was stupid.

"She's not my friend," Zoey said.

"So you *did* push her."

"No," Zoey said, shaking her head sharply as anger rushed through her. "No!" she repeated. She felt panic rise, bitter in her throat. They thought she was responsible — that she'd killed Audra! "She attacked me. She was crazy."

"Uh-huh," said the officer, taking notes. He raised his eyebrows at his partner. They clearly thought Zoey was lying. "What were you doing at the lake?"

Zoey stood up. She had to make them believe her. "We were . . . I was — she was stalking my brother!" Zoey blurted, knowing *she* was the one who sounded insane. "Tom . . . I had to find him, and —"

"Thanks, boys. I'll take it from here." A deep, familiar voice interrupted Zoey's babbling, and she felt a heavy hand on her shoulder. She looked up into the dark, piercing eyes of her father.

"DA Ramirez!" The head cop took a step back. "We were just —"

"I can see that," the district attorney said calmly, plucking the notebook from the other officer's hands. He ripped off the top sheet and tucked it neatly into his suit pocket before handing the notebook back to the stunned cop. "I appreciate what you've done here, but there is no need for further questioning. I'm sure you didn't realize that Zoey is my daughter."

The officers' jaws dropped. For once Zoey didn't mind letting her father take over. She slipped behind him, feeling almost comforted.

"You will leave Zoey out of your report," DA Ramirez told the officers. He spoke so calmly it was almost hypnotic — and the policemen were clearly under the DA's spell. "She's a minor. I don't want to see her name in the paper. Understood?"

The officers nodded.

When Zoey heard the word "paper" the feeling of being protected disappeared as quickly as it had enveloped her. *Of course.* Her dad wasn't looking out for her, he was looking out for himself and his political career. DA Ramirez was planning to run for Congress the next fall, and his budding campaign was all he cared about. Zoey should have known right away that he was only worried she might sully his reputation.

"Can we go home?" Zoey asked her dad without looking at him. She wanted to get out of there. She wasn't sure how much longer her legs or her stomach would hold up.

The DA held up a hand to silence his daughter and went on talking to the cops. Only Zoey seemed to notice as Audra's body was wheeled out from behind the curtains. The dead girl was hidden by a sheet, but one pale arm dangled disturbingly over the side of the gurney.

"Oh, God." Zoey put her hand over her mouth and tried not to hurl. Her dad ignored her, but an officer pointed down the brightly lit hall. "Bathroom's that way," he said easily. Zoey lurched in the direction the cop had pointed. *Please don't let it be far.* As soon as she started moving, the nausea faded. But the weakness in her knees and the pounding in her head continued to overwhelm her. Leaning on the rail that lined the hallway, she paused.

"Do you go to Stafford?"

"What?" Zoey looked up. A guy wearing a camera and an orange vest stood right behind her.

"Do you go to Stafford Academy?" he asked again. From the look of him Zoey guessed he was a reporter. She nodded yes, wishing she hadn't paused on her way to the restroom.

"So you know the boy in the coma?"

That caught Zoey's attention, fast. "What boy?" she demanded, grabbing the reporter's arm. "Who is it?"

Zoey's pulse raced. *Please don't say Tom. Please don't say Tom.* But he didn't have to say it — she *knew* it must be her twin. She'd rushed off with Audra to try to save him from destruction. Now Audra was dead. And Tom . . .

"All I know is there's a Stafford boy unconscious in the ICU," the reporter said. "There was a fight at the school, and —"

"Who is it?" Zoey shouted, giving the guy a shake. "What's his name?"

The reporter pulled out of her grasp. "Whoa, calm down. I was asking *you*." He gave her a look like she was out of her head, but Zoey never saw it. She was running as fast as she could toward the intensive care unit.

Chapter Two

Zoey sprinted down the long hall. She had no idea which direction the ICU was in, but she was going to get there fast. The silver buckles on her Cesare Paciotti boots jingled as she careened down the nearly empty corridor, searching for a nurses' station or a sign or some-one to give her directions. Patients stared at her as she passed. Luckily, nobody tried to stop her. She looked right and left into the rooms as she flew by, hoping to spot Tom. The faces that gazed back at her were all unfamiliar.

Zoey resisted the urge to shout her brother's name. The more seconds that passed, the more panicked she felt. She choked back tears. Her vision blurred.

"Zoey?"

Wiping her eyes, Zoey turned and looked into the face of her best friend, Alison Rose. Zoey had never felt so happy to see anyone in her life. She hugged Alison tightly.

"What . . . how . . ." Zoey struggled to speak. Alison pressed her lips together as a tear ran down her cheek. She looked tired and totally strung out — like she had been crying for days.

"Chad," Alison choked out. "Chad's in a coma." She collapsed back on Zoey.

It's not Tom. Zoey felt relief wash over her as Alison sobbed against her. *Thank goodness it's not Tom.*

"They don't know what's wrong." Alison's voice was muffled in Zoey's sweater. "And they don't know if he'll ever wake up. He and Tom had a big fight in the hall, and then . . ." Alison was crying too hard to go on.

Zoey squeezed her tightly. As the relief subsided, the reality of what Alison was saying began to sink in.

11

"Oh, Alison," Zoey said. "I'm so, so sorry."

Alison and Chad had broken up a couple of months ago, and it hadn't been pretty. Even though Chad was now going out with Alison's ex-best friend and cousin, Kelly, it was no secret to Zoey that Alison still had feelings for him. Chad was also Tom's best friend, and Zoey knew her brother would be taking this news just as hard as Alison.

"So, if you didn't know about Chad . . . what are you doing here?" Alison asked, searching her friend's face.

"Audra's dead," Zoey said bluntly. She slid down the wall until she was sitting on the cold tile floor. "I watched her die."

Alison's eyes grew wide and she dropped down next to Zoey. "Oh, my God," she breathed. "What happened?"

"I was looking for Tom. Audra told me she knew where he was, so I got in the car with her and —"

Zoey stopped talking when she spotted the reporter in the orange vest coming around the corner of the hall.

Zoey stood quickly. "Reporter," she said to Alison, nodding in the guy's direction. "Let's go."

Alison ducked her head and was on her feet in an instant. She motioned to Zoey that they should head for the restroom. As the daughter of domestic tycoon and tabloid favorite Helen Rose and the granddaughter of Silver Spring's wealthiest citizen, Tamara Diamond, Alison knew how to dodge the press. She'd spent way too much time doing just that since her mother had been arrested and charged with tax fraud, grand larceny, and embezzlement. The high-profile trial was only a week away, and Zoey knew Alison couldn't wait for the whole thing to just be over — whether or not it meant her mother's release from jail.

"There you are." Zoey heard her father's voice and looked back over her shoulder. The DA was coming toward them. He pushed past the reporter and took Zoey by the arm. His touch was unyielding — there was no shaking free of his grasp. But it was not unkind, and Zoey

13

could not deny she needed an escort out of there.

"It's time to go," Zoey's dad rumbled. Zoey stumbled along beside him, turning back to mouth a silent "sorry" to Alison before her friend disappeared into the bathroom.

Chapter Three

Tom crouched behind a shrub outside the main entrance to Silver Spring General Hospital. The position made his knees ache, and his hands were numb with cold, but he didn't care. He was almost beyond feeling — physical feeling, anyway. Emotionally, he was feeling too much. A lot too much.

He had been waiting outside the hospital for most of the afternoon, watching people go in and out. He wanted to go in to see Chad. He really did. But he felt frozen, unable to move.

It had only been a couple of hours since he had shoved Chad against the lockers, delivering the blow that had landed his friend in the hospital — but it felt like an eternity. Maybe because Tom hadn't stopped reliving it in his head.

The fight had been building for a long time. Tom was sick of helping Chad cheat so he could retain his scholarship — the one nobody except the two of them knew about. But mostly, Tom had to admit, the fight was about Kelly. Tom had made a play for his best friend's girl. It went against every rule in the unspoken guy code of ethics. But he had done it. And of course Chad had gotten mad. Who wouldn't?

The fight hadn't lasted long. When Chad fell, Tom stormed off to tell the dean that Stafford's secret charity case was a liar and a cheat. But the dean wasn't there, and while Tom was waiting, steaming, a couple of kids had rushed in with the news that Chad was in a coma.

"I did this," Tom said aloud, clenching his fists. "And now I have to face it." Tom was about to emerge from the bushes when the hospital doors slid open and his father and sister stepped out of the building.

What the —? Tom ducked back down, but even if he hadn't, he didn't think they would have seen him. His dad had an "all business" look on his face, and Zoey looked like a zombie. *Why are* they *here?* Tom wondered.

He stared at his family. Next to their dad, Zoey looked extra tiny. Had she lost weight since coming home to Silver Spring? Tom squinted in the afternoon light. Zoey definitely had circles under her eyes that were not makeup.

Tom wished he could get her attention, get her away from their dad. Talk to her. Why had he cut her off? He could barely remember. As he watched Zoey climb into the car with the DA, a small part of him wished he was safe in the car, too, headed home. He was probably going to be in serious trouble for all of this. Tom was ready to face that, all of it. *After* he saw Chad. Right now he was here for his best friend — like he should have been all along.

When his father's silver Lexus LX was gone, Tom stood up, stepped onto the path, and walked through the sliding doors. The smell of antiseptic and illness assaulted his nose. His stomach protested, and it occurred to Tom that he had not eaten since breakfast. It felt like it had been years since he had rolled out of bed that morning.

"Chad Simon's room, please," Tom said as he stepped up to the information desk.

"Sorry, family only in the ICU." The guy at the info station was wearing superbright Hawaiian-print scrubs. They hurt Tom's eyes.

"Can you just tell me where he's located?" Tom said, trying to be patient.

"I said you can't go in."

Tom's anger flared, but he doused it quickly. Anger had only been getting him into trouble lately.

"Look, I just want to talk to his family," Tom said as calmly as he could.

The guy nodded. "Intensive care is at the end of the hall. He's in room one twenty-eight."

"Thanks." Tom's heart sped up as he followed the arrows toward the ICU. He wondered what he was going to say to Chad when he saw him. *Will he be able to hear me? Will he be able to forgive me?*

Tom's pace slowed as he got closer. His eyes narrowed in on the numbers 1-2-8 next to the closed wooden door. He stared at the digits until everything around them started to turn black. He took a step back and was practically treading on Alison before he realized she was sitting against the wall.

"Oh."

"Oh." Alison looked up at Tom. Her eyes were red. Tom noticed a spot of blood on her clothes. She must have been with Chad when . . .

"Um . . . your dad and Zoey just left." Alison pointed back the way Tom had come.

"Uh, um, yeah. I saw them." Tom nodded. Then as an afterthought he added, "What were they doing here?"

"They didn't tell you?" Alison was searching Tom's face. Tom felt his cheeks redden under her gaze. He wondered if she blamed him for what happened to Chad.

Tom shook his head. "Tell me what?"

Alison bit her lip. "Audra . . ." she said finally. "She's dead."

If there hadn't been a handrail on the wall, Tom might have fallen over. *Audra dead?* "What?" he blurted. It had to be a mistake.

"I'm sorry. I don't know the details. But Zoey was with her. She was looking for you," Alison said gently. "I was waiting here to see Chad . . . and . . ." She gestured across the hall at the closed door of Chad's room and drew a shuddering breath. "They've been wheeling him in and out for tests. His family is with him, but . . . he's not waking up. He's just lying there. I guess he hit his head when you . . ." Alison stopped talking and looked away from Tom.

Tom felt the lump in his throat grow, threatening to block off his airway. Audra was dead. Zoey had been with her. Chad was in a coma. It was all his fault, and Alison knew it. What must she think of him? At the moment Tom didn't know what he thought of himself.

For a long time Tom and Alison stood staring at the floor, not speaking. Their silence was finally interrupted by the confident click-click-clicking of high-heeled boots on the tile floor.

When Kelly Reeves rounded the corner, Tom inhaled sharply. Watching Kelly stride toward him, shaking her golden hair back over her shoulders, he had to resist the urge to turn away. As he looked into Kelly's smoldering eyes he knew exactly why he had done it. He knew why he had treated Chad so badly, why he'd risked everything, including their friendship. And he knew he would do it again if he had the chance. The reason was simple: Kelly. Kelly could make anyone do anything just for the opportunity to be near her.

Maybe if Chad ever woke up, he'd understand. Maybe he could forgive Tom. After all, Chad knew what it was like to be under Kelly's spell, to choose her over everything else. That's why he had dumped Alison to be with her.

Kelly's heels clicked to a halt beside Tom just as the door to room 128 opened. Chad's mother appeared on the other side, looking exhausted. Her eyes were even redder than Alison's. Her husband and Chad's older brother, Dustin, stepped out into the hall, too, followed by a doctor.

Tom wished he could melt into the floor. He wished Dustin would punch him. That Mrs. Simon would slap him, or Mr. Simon would yell. But the Simon family greeted him with sad smiles. Apparently nobody had told them about the fight. "You can go in," Chad's mom said softly to Tom. "I'm sure Chad would love to see you." Her voice cracked and she quickly buried her head in her husband's shoulder. Tom turned away and walked into Chad's room so he would not have to see her cry.

Chapter Four

This is it. Alison closed her eyes and took a deep breath to calm her racing heart. The door was finally open, room 128 was right in front of her, and she could finally see Chad. Only one thing still stood in her way.

Kelly. Alison's best-friend-turned-nemesis had struck a pose, right in the middle of the doorway. So typical. Kelly was the last to arrive and the first in line.

Alison could not help but notice that her cousin was wearing a different skirt than the one she'd had on at school, and new Anna Sui boots. Freshly applied eye shadow shimmered on her lids as she gave Alison's rumpled outfit a once-over and made a face.

"Gross," Kelly said, eyeing the bloodstain on Alison's shirt. "You're a mess, Al. I can't believe Grandmother Diamond lets you go out like that."

Alison glared back. She did not care that she had Chad's dried blood on her. It was a badge of honor, because she had been there with him. *She* had never left him. *She* had stayed by his side, or as close as she could get, since this nightmare had started.

"So sorry," Alison hissed sarcastically. "I didn't have time to shower and change. I thought Chad might need me."

"Why would he need *you*?" Kelly asked, giving her a "you're so pathetic" look. "He has *me*."

Alison balled her hands into fists, shoved them in her pockets, and willed herself to stay calm. She could not let Kelly get to her. Not here. Not now. She was here for Chad. Chad was all that mattered.

Taking a deep breath, Alison followed Kelly into Chad's room. What she saw made her gasp.

Chad was lying deathly still on the hospital bed surrounded by beeping and pinging machines. He had wires taped to his chest and tubes coming out of his arms, attached to his finger, and poking out of his gown. He looked like a marionette waiting for someone to pull his strings. His face was almost peaceful, and Alison saw his eyelids flutter — like he was dreaming and about to wake up. She willed his big brown eyes to open, to smile into hers. They didn't.

Unable to look away, Alison watched as Chad's chest rose and fell slowly. He was breathing on his own. That was something. But he looked incredibly pale against the crisp white sheets, and as fragile as the thin blue gown they had dressed him in.

Tearing her eyes away from Chad, Alison looked to see Kelly's reaction. The girl could not hide her distaste. Her nose was wrinkled as she gingerly picked her way past the IV and stationed herself in the only chair in the room — right next to Chad's bedside. Tom stood in one corner, biting his lip. Alison picked a spot in the other corner. She stood still, waiting for the curly-haired boy on the bed — *her* boy — to awaken. The last words he had spoken before he'd collapsed echoed in her head. *I still love you.* Her heart ached at the thought, and she wished once more that she'd gotten the chance to tell him that she still loved him, too. She hoped more than anything that she wasn't too late.

Fighting back tears for the hundredth time that day, Alison remembered the moment when Chad's eyes had gone dark and he'd slipped away from her. It had been the scariest moment of Alison's life. It was worse than watching her mother's arrest. Worse than when Kelly had first betrayed her. Worse than the moment she'd realized her father had disappeared. Worse than realizing there was nobody in her family she could truly trust — that they were all too wrapped up in their secrets and money and lies.

Chad's love wasn't like that. It was simple and pure. His love was real.

Alison had lost Chad to Kelly once already. But now that she knew his heart was still hers, she vowed that she would never lose it again. It didn't matter that Kelly was Chad's girlfriend now. *Alison* was the one he loved.

Alison patiently stood waiting for Kelly to get bored and go home — she was sure it would not take long. But the girl was putting on a good show, stroking Chad's hand (the one without the IV), and calling his name. She wished Tom would leave, too, even though he was just standing there staring. She wanted to be alone with Chad. Even if he couldn't hear her, she needed to tell him how she felt.

"You know, since I'm here now, it would be all right if you wanted to run along and change," Kelly said pointedly.

"That's okay," Alison replied sweetly. "I want to make sure Chad sees someone he loves when he wakes up."

"Hello?" Kelly gestured toward herself and gave Alison an icy stare.

Tom coughed awkwardly, and Alison suddenly felt relieved that he was there. If he wasn't, Kelly would *really* be going after her.

Ignoring Kelly, Alison gave Tom a weak smile. She'd thought he looked pretty bad when she saw him in the hall. But standing in Chad's room she realized he looked terrible. His rumpled clothes were not a good sign. But it was his expression that really worried Alison. His dark eyes stared at Chad with a look she could only describe as total and complete agony. The guy had lost two of his closest friends in one day — and one of them was *dead*.

Alison briefly considered trying to comfort Tom, or at least telling him she was sorry about Audra. But when she opened her mouth to speak she found she couldn't. First of all, what could she possibly say? And second, even though she knew that deep down Tom was a good guy, he had been totally out of control lately. He had been terrible to Zoey, flying off the handle at the stupidest things and letting his temper flare. If Chad was in this condition because Tom couldn't keep his anger in check, well, then maybe he *should* feel guilty.

The door opened and Mr. and Mrs. Simon slipped back into the room. Alison heard a commotion in the hall. She peered through the open doorway and saw the guy who she assumed was Chad's brother, Dustin, flailing and cursing. Two nurses were trying to calm him down, but Dustin wasn't having it. He shook them off like flies and punched a wall, hard. Alison cringed.

"Dustin's very upset," Chad's mother said, half apologizing, as the nurses led him away.

"We all are," his dad choked.

Kelly made a little sobbing sound to get everyone's attention focused back on her.

"Oh, Mrs. Simon, I'm so sorry you have to go through this." Kelly stood up and held out her hand. "I'm Kelly, Chad's girlfriend."

Mrs. Simon shook Kelly's hand awkwardly. She wore glasses and had mousy brown hair pulled back in a ponytail.

"I'm Alison," Alison offered. *The girl your son loves*, she added in her head. Mrs. Simon took Alison's hand, too. Her grasp was weak and her hands were cold. Struggling to find something comforting to say, all Alison could think of was the one thing Chad had ever told her about his parents — that they never stopped fighting.

"Is there any news?" Now that her audience had doubled, Kelly had moved in closer to Chad and was really milking it. Alison resisted the urge to slap her.

"The doctors think he'll wake up," Mr. Simon said, "but they don't know when. The tests show some sort of head trauma, which could account for the coma —"

Glancing at Tom, Alison watched the blood drain from his face.

"But there's something else. His red blood cell count is low. His lymph nodes are swollen. We're not certain yet, but . . ." Mr. Simon paused, and his wife released a quick, deep sob. "They think he might have Hodgkin's disease. Cancer of the lymph nodes."

Hodgkin's disease. Alison's heart sank and her eyes welled with tears. The boy she loved had cancer.

"That's horrible," Kelly gasped. She held her hands over her face, but Alison could tell she wasn't crying. Tom had dry eyes, too, but was shaking like a leaf.

"I should have known," Tom said softly. Then he grabbed Mr. Simon's shoulder. "He's been having headaches . . . lots of them. I should have told somebody." Tom released Mr. Simon and started to pace in the tiny room. "And he lost weight. You noticed, right?" He looked Chad's mom in the eye. Alison could tell she was on the verge of collapse, and Tom's outburst wasn't helping. "Why didn't I say anything? Why didn't I do anything?" Tom was howling now.

Alison put her hand on his arm and led him back to the corner. "I should have done something," Tom kept repeating.

"There was no way to know." Alison kept her hand on Tom's arm. She felt oddly relieved that the coma was not his fault, and terrified because the cancer that caused it was so much scarier. "None of us saw this coming, not even Chad." Alison spoke softly. "All we can do now is wait."

Chapter Five

Wow. Kelly kept her face hidden in her hands and listened to Tom freak out. He was totally blaming himself. It almost made her feel bad. Except this wasn't about *him*. She released a sob. It was time to refocus the drama.

A gentle touch on her shoulder made Kelly look up. She saw the sympathetic eyes of Chad's mother gazing down at her. Kelly dabbed her eyes as Mr. Simon circled to her other side. Chad's parents comforting *her*! This was more like it. After all, Chad was their son, and *her* boyfriend. As far as Kelly was concerned, Tom and Alison belonged in the waiting room.

Mr. Simon gave Kelly an awkward pat

on the head. "He'll be just fine," he said unconvincingly.

"Of course he will." Kelly sniffed. *But could you watch the hair?* She turned slightly and noticed a tag sticking out of the back of Mrs. Simon's burnt-orange mock turtleneck. Kelly blinked. Was she actually wearing *L.L. Bean*?

Ensconced in the Simon family sympathy huddle, Kelly gave Mrs. Simon the once-over, eyeing her khakis and the heart pendant dangling from a silver chain around her neck. Total mall wear. Had she borrowed her clothes and jewelry from her housekeeper?

Thank God my mom doesn't go out in public like that, Kelly thought. Sure, her mother's taste left a lot to be desired, but at least she never looked low-rent. Mrs. Simon was obviously in desperate need of a personal shopper.

Kelly glanced over at the Diesel jeans and soft blue sweater Chad had been wearing when he collapsed. Even draped over a chair, they looked acceptable. And so did the clothes on the hot angry brother in the hallway. The college one . . . definitely a touch scruffy, but in a hipster sort of way.

"We'll get through this . . . together," Kelly said, flashing Chad's parents a heartbroken smile. Kelly turned to look at her comatose boyfriend. She'd had no idea that Chad had an older brother — until quite recently she hadn't even known about the younger one. She felt a flash of newfound respect. *Chad certainly has his share of little secrets. . . .*

Speaking of secrets . . . "Where's Will?" Kelly asked Chad's mother. She kept her voice low so Alison wouldn't overhear the question. Chad had never told Alison about his autistic little brother, and Kelly wanted to keep Chad's secret — until the time was right to spring it on Alison herself.

Mrs. Simon sniffled. "Will can't handle hospitals," she explained into her tissue. "It's just too much for him. And if he saw Chad like . . . this . . ."

Kelly opened her arms and Mrs. Simon collapsed into them. "There, there," she said, patting Chad's mother's back. Normally she wouldn't dream of letting a stranger snot up her sweater, but she could feel Alison watching from her spot in the corner, and she wanted her cousin to get an eyeful of the cozy scene. Besides, she'd just give the sweater to the housekeeper to have it dry-cleaned.

As Mrs. Simon cried and Alison seethed, Kelly congratulated herself on how well she'd worked the situation. She was slipping into the role of coma-victim's girlfriend as easily as a size-two Stella McCartney. She could tell already that this whole thing would turn out well for her. It was pretty ironic, really. If Chad hadn't blacked out right when he did, he and Kelly would definitely be over. But as long as Chad was comatose, it seemed he was worth keeping. First on the list of benefits was how Kelly's presence by Chad's bedside was torturing Alison.

Nobody besides Kelly and Alison knew that Chad had confessed his love to Alison just seconds before he went comatose. And as long as Chad was like this, nobody had to find out. *Poor little Al*, Kelly thought as she caught her cousin's blue eyes and flashed her a cruel smile. Alison looked away and tucked a lock of dark hair behind her ear. *She was so close to getting what she wants. So close, and yet so far.*

Chad would never be Alison's again — Kelly would make sure of that.

Working up a small sob, Kelly put her hand to her mouth and pretended to get all choked up. "You . . . you should have heard him just before he blacked out," she told Mrs. Simon, making sure Alison was getting every word. "He was talking complete nonsense. I didn't know what to do. I just stayed by his side until the medics tore him away from me."

Alison's head jerked up and Kelly met her gaze. In that room only Kelly, Alison, and Chad knew the truth. And Chad wasn't talking.

Chapter Six

Crunch, crunch, crunch. Slowly Zoey ground her toast to bits between her teeth, bracing herself for the storm. She was not sure what she was dreading more, going to school or her father's inevitable lecture.

Ever since her father had picked her up at the hospital the day before, Zoey had been waiting for him to let her have it — to launch into one of his infamous tirades about her keeping her nose clean, staying out of trouble, toeing the line, protecting her reputation. But the blistering, vein-popping scream-fest hadn't come. Hearing heavy footsteps in the hall, Zoey stopped chewing. This was it. But DA Daddy just breezed into the kitchen and headed straight for his morning coffee without even acknowledging his daughter. It was excruciating. Zoey wished he'd just scream already and get it over with.

"Good morning," Zoey said quietly. She thought about thanking her dad for bailing her out the night before, but then thought better of it. *He did it for his own benefit*, she reminded herself, *not mine*. Still, she was glad he'd shown up. She scraped a blackened bit off her toast with a butter knife and watched her dad pick up the paper.

There, Zoey thought. *Here it comes*. The headline was sure to set him off: STAFFORD DOUBLE TRAGEDY: ONE STUDENT DEAD, ANOTHER IN COMA. The news was so big that it had bumped the usual top story — Alison's mother's upcoming trial — to the second page.

But as her father read the article, his expression remained completely unaltered.

Zoey shoved her plate away. Her appetite was toast. She wished her dad would say something, anything. The silence was worse than any rampage. She knew that underneath the calm mask he had to be mad. A girl was dead, and Zoey had been the only witness. If word got out about her involvement, it was sure to damage her father's reputation, and compromise his upcoming congressional campaign. If only her father would launch into it already — tell her how badly she'd screwed up, how stupid she had been. Then maybe she could start to feel better.

I shouldn't have been there, Zoey told herself. *She shouldn't be dead.* If only she hadn't argued with Audra. If only she'd walked away instead of trying to make Audra be rational. If only she had caught her hand. . . . *There are too many if's.*

Zoey pushed back her chair and stood — she couldn't sit in that silent kitchen any longer. She was dumping her dishes into the sink when Deirdre, Zoey and Tom's new stepmother, bounced in. "Hey there!" she squeaked. "What's for breakfast?"

"Scrambled brain with a side of the silent treatment," Zoey muttered. Her father's wife was so perky, Zoey was starting to suspect she breathed helium.

"What, honey?" Deirdre asked, tilting her head like a cocker spaniel.

"Never mind," Zoey mumbled.

"Whatcha reading? Anything new?" Deirdre kissed her husband on the top of the head, making him flinch. He grunted but didn't answer her questions. Clearly Zoey's dad had not shared any "news" with her about yesterday. Nor had he gotten beyond the front-page article. Usually he skimmed the paper, flipping through it quickly. He preferred to get his news from the radio in his car — the DA did not care to stay in one place too long. But today's headline had obviously caught his interest — he hadn't turned a single page.

Zoey had to look away from the weird family scene. Was that the smell of her father's blood boiling, or was it just the awful protein-laced chocolate diet shake Deirdre was whipping up? If only Tom was here to share this cozy moment.

"Where's Tommy?" Deirdre asked, reading Zoey's mind.

"In bed," Zoey's dad answered with a grunt.

"Ooh. He's going to be late for school!"

Deirdre fussed, dumping some vile-looking powder into the blender. "I'll go wake him up."

"Just leave him be," the DA ordered. "He's taking a mental-health day."

Whoa. Zoey could barely believe her ears. It was downright human of her father to cut Tom a little slack — and not exactly par for the course. Tom and their dad had been butting heads big-time lately. But given the circumstances . . .

Zoey knew from Alison's text message that they'd both stayed by Chad's bedside until the nurses kicked them out. Afterward she'd heard him pacing half the night in his room — he hadn't slept, and neither had she.

Zoey longed to stay home, too, to skip school and maybe even find a chance to talk to her brother. She wanted to know how he was doing . . . and to tell him what had happened with Audra. Zoey was seriously missing the days before their mom had died and she was shipped off to boarding school — the days when she and Tom had been tight. A day alone together in the house might help them start to reconnect, and the sooner they did that the better. They needed each other.

When her shake was mixed up, Deirdre went back upstairs to get started on her shimmy. She liked to sip and do StairMaster in front of the morning talk shows.

Finally, Zoey's father looked up from the paper and spoke. "They kept your name out. Just like I asked them to." His voice was monotone. His expression was as blank as if he'd been telling her the weather forecast. Getting to his feet, he crossed the kitchen and dropped the newspaper in front of Zoey on the counter before walking out.

Zoey shivered. She felt . . . slimy. No. She felt guilty. "Just like I asked them to," he had said. *Just like I have something to hide*, Zoey thought with a shudder. This was worse than a lecture, worse than the silent treatment. She and her dad were in cahoots.

Chapter Seven

Zoey dragged her feet through the fallen leaves that littered the walkway leading to Stafford Academy. She was in no hurry to climb the marble stairs and enter the two-story brick building. If it weren't for her father's car still idling in the parking lot, or her best friend waiting inside, Zoey would have been running, screaming in the opposite direction. She knew what everyone at Stafford would be talking about — Chad . . . and Audra.

At least nobody knows I was there, Zoey consoled herself. It was a small comfort. Giving the leaves a last kick, Zoey pulled open the wide door and stepped into the hallway, hoping she could find Alison quickly.

Zoey ducked her head and walked past the clusters of students talking, crying, and hugging in the halls. She picked up bits of conversation as she went.

"There's no way it was suicide."

"She had so much to live for."

"They're canceling classes."

"Did you hear he has cancer?"

"I heard she was pushed."

The rumors were flying. And the mood at Stafford was even creepier than the vibe at her house. Some of the kids seemed struck dumb by the news, wandering the hallways numb with disbelief. Others were wailing loudly, being comforted by friends. Zoey was halfway between being annoyed at the wailers and feeling jealous, wishing she could break down, too. What did any of them know? They weren't even there.

Right in front of her locker, Zoey spotted three girls from the debate team, Carlie, Gina, and Amber. Gina was standing in between the other two girls. She was crying so hard she could barely breathe. But when she spotted Zoey, she stopped sobbing.

Typical, Zoey thought. *Now that Audra's dead, Gina can't live without her — even though they were barely even friends.*

"There she is," Gina hissed, wiping her nose.

Carlie and Amber turned to glare at Zoey. Amber wrapped an arm protectively over Gina's shoulders.

"It was you, wasn't it?" Gina said accusingly.

Zoey's heart raced. "I'm really sorry abou —"

"Don't play dumb," Carlie sneered. "We know you were there."

"Amber saw you get into her car, so don't try to deny it." Shrugging off Amber's arm, Gina took a step toward Zoey. "You got into her car and now she's dead." Gina's voice cracked, making Zoey flinch. She looked down at her feet.

"So you don't deny it?" Amber demanded.

"Deny what? I didn't kill her, if that's what you mean." Zoey's voice was louder than she meant it to be and several heads in the hall turned to look. "She was crazy," Zoey tried again. Gina's face crumpled and she collapsed into Amber and Carlie's arms.

Zoey felt her face redden and her eyes blur. She stepped past the girls to her locker, but she couldn't see the numbers on her lock clearly. She spun the dial around and around, hoping the combination would magically click into place.

Zoey suddenly felt like she was going to throw up, and she knew exactly why. She may not have killed her, but in her heart of hearts she *did* hate Audra — hated her for what she'd done to Tom. Audra hadn't just stalked Tom. She'd reeled him into her web of insanity and turned him against everyone who'd cared about him. She had sunk her claws in when Tom was at his most vulnerable, and she'd made it clear she would never let go. Tom wasn't a person to Audra — he was a possession. It made Zoey sick to admit it, but she was relieved that the crazy girl was gone.

Swallowing hard, Zoey focused on the dial. She had to get her locker open, get her stuff, and get out of there.

Finally Zoey got the metal door open. But behind her, Audra's friends were still gathered.

"Burning down a school wasn't enough?"

Carlie practically shouted. "You had to *kill* someone, too?"

Zoey turned slowly to face them. For the first time, she noticed that they were all wearing black armbands. They glared at Zoey with utter hatred. "Look, I didn't kill her," she said quietly. "She lunged at me and slipped over the edge. *She* was trying to kill *me*."

There was dead silence in the halls. Everyone was watching the confrontation now. Zoey scanned the crowd for a single look of sympathy or belief. She saw nothing. And then Amber, Carlie, and Gina pressed closer, blocking Zoey's path. Amber came so close Zoey could see the tear streaks on her cheeks.

"I know you hated her," Amber screamed. "I know you couldn't stand that she was smarter than you. Audra was my friend — and I know you killed her. But you won't get away with it." Zoey stared at the girl, completely stunned. Amber seemed near hysterics. Zoey just wanted to bolt — coming to school had been a huge mistake — but the debate team had her surrounded. She was trapped.

Overhead the PA system crackled and the

dean's voice echoed in the corridor. "In light of the recent tragedies, students are to report to the auditorium for a special assembly. All regular classes are canceled. Please report to the auditorium for further announcements."

The halls began to buzz again, but the debate team didn't budge. Zoey looked around frantically for a way out.

And then, out of the blue, Alison broke through the crowd and took Zoey by the elbow. "Leave her alone," she said plainly. And without so much as a pause, Alison pushed through the mass of people, pulling Zoey down the hall and into the girls' bathroom.

As soon as the door closed behind her, Zoey burst into tears. She felt Alison's arms wrap around her and cried even harder.

"We were arguing about Tom," Zoey said, desperate for Alison to know the truth. "She was acting crazy, taunting me with the car keys, and saying how Tom *belongs* to her and how much he hated me, that I was ruining his life. She was laughing when she lunged at me. Only I dodged, and . . ." Zoey paused as her eyes filled with tears.

Alison's eyes were huge, but there was not even a crumb of doubt in her expression — only sympathy and understanding. Wiping her eyes, Zoey drew a ragged breath. She realized how good it felt to tell someone — someone who knew she was telling the truth. Alison really was a lifesaver, and not just today. Zoey looked at her friend gratefully and noticed for the first time how awful *she* looked.

"But enough about me." Zoey forced a smile. "How are you doing?" she asked, gently putting a hand on Alison's arm. "Any changes with Chad?"

Alison shook her head. "No changes," she said sadly. "Unless you count the fact that Kelly is acting like she actually cares about him and is officially best friends with his parents!" Alison's tone was light, but she blinked back tears.

"That snake," Zoey scowled.

"I keep telling myself it doesn't matter because as soon as Chad wakes up, and I tell him I love him, too, he's gonna kick her to the curb. Just as soon as he wakes up . . ." Alison's eyes began to fill with tears again.

"Let's get out of here." Zoey grabbed Alison's

hand and pulled her out the bathroom door. A few final students shuffled somberly toward the auditorium.

"I don't think I can handle the assembly." Alison sniffed.

Zoey pulled her friend more firmly down the hall. "I mean *really* get out of here," she said. "We're going to Hardwired. Coffee. My treat."

Alison nodded and Zoey led the way to the nearest exit.

Chapter Eight

Tom rolled over in bed with a giant stretch. His curtains were open, and late-morning sun streamed across the floor of his room. The house was totally quiet. For a whole minute, Tom felt great. Then everything came flooding back in a massive, ugly torrent.

Tom looked at the clock. It was almost eleven. He had basically been in bed for two days, only getting up to call the hospital, pee, and eat the food Deirdre left outside his door. Grabbing the phone next to his bed, Tom sat up and hit REDIAL. A nurse picked up on the first ring.

"ICU."

"Um, hi. I was calling to check on a patient

there . . . Chad Simon. Is he still . . . has he . . . ?" Tom had called and asked the same question a half dozen times since Wednesday but it was still hard to do.

"He's still stable. There have been no changes," the nurse said gently.

"Thank you," Tom mumbled before hanging up the phone and flopping back down on his bed.

Tom shut his eyes. He wished he could go back to sleep forever. He was still exhausted from the tossing and turning, from the unending nightmares. But even that was better than being awake.

Too bad I'm not the one in the coma, he thought glibly. Then the guilt overwhelmed him. His best friend was dead to the world because of him.

Tom shakily got to his feet. He hadn't been eating much — just the energy bars and canned protein drinks Deirdre left him. She also left a note saying the dean had called an emergency school closing to give kids some time to cope with what was happening.

Grabbing some clothes, he shuffled down the

hall to take a shower. Getting clean ought to help a little — the funky smell he was sporting certainly wasn't easing his nausea any. Then he'd grab something to eat and head to the hospital. By the time he got there Chad might be doing better. Maybe he would even be awake. . . .

Tom pushed open the bathroom door and nearly bumped into Zoey, who was standing at the sink brushing her teeth. One glance at her and Tom knew she wasn't doing so great, either. A fresh wave of guilt pummeled his sore conscience. Tom was so obsessed with Chad that he had been pushing thoughts about Audra to the back of his mind. It did not seem possible that she was dead. It seemed even more improbable that Zoey was there when it happened — and all because of him.

"Hey," Zoey mumbled, her mouth full of toothpaste foam. Tom met her gaze and was surprised to discover that her expression was full of compassion.

Standing in the doorway, looking at his twin, Tom remembered the last time he'd felt this horrible. It was about five years ago, right after their mom died. Chad in a coma and Audra dead didn't quite compare to losing his mom, but there were similarities for sure. The sick feeling. The numbness. The guilt for still being alive and okay.

Tom watched Zoey spit into the sink. When their mom died, Zoey was the one who was there with him. The one he talked to. The one he cried with. He could not have made it through that nightmare without her.

Suddenly Tom couldn't remember why he had been so angry with Zoey, why he'd been shutting her out so hard.

Tom opened his mouth to speak, not sure what he was going to say or where to start. "I'm s-sorry about Audra," he stammered, surprising himself.

From Zoey's expression, Tom could tell that he'd surprised her as well. She rinsed her toothbrush and took a sip of water. "I'm sorry, too," she said.

Tom nodded in agreement, feeling immensely grateful that she did not seem to be holding a grudge, and that she was still speaking to him. Because they had a lot of talking to do.

Chapter Nine

Zoey couldn't believe what she was seeing — or hearing. For the first time since she'd come back to Silver Spring, her twin brother looked . . . open. Totally wounded, yes. But not angry or resentful. He actually seemed like he might be on Zoey's side.

Zoey had been reaching out to her brother for ages, with zero results. Negative zero, actually. This little crack in his veneer was a chance Zoey was not going to pass up.

"So, uh, if you ever want to talk . . ." she said quietly, looking into Tom's face.

"Actually, I . . ." Tom trailed off as he leaned his athletic frame against the open door and looked at the ceiling. Zoey waited patiently for him to go on.

"I think you were right about Audra. I mean, I think she was crazy."

Zoey nodded but didn't say anything. She had the feeling that Tom wasn't finished.

"But she was, well, she was always there for me. And she listened. I could tell her anything and she didn't judge."

"She judged me," Zoey said quietly.

"I know," Tom admitted, staring at the tile floor. "She really did hate you. But that doesn't mean . . ."

". . . that she deserved to die," Zoey finished in a low voice. "I didn't kill her. You know that, right?"

Tom's head jerked up. "Of course I do," he said slowly. There was a long pause. "Do you want to talk about it?"

Zoey shrugged. She did, and then she didn't. "She took me to the lake." Zoey shuddered.

"Mom's lake," Tom said. "She took me there, too."

Zoey nodded. "On the bridge, she totally

flipped out and lunged at me. I had no idea it was coming."

Zoey blinked fast and looked away from her brother's face.

"She loved that lake," Tom said. "I think she felt really free there."

"It's totally surreal," Zoey said. "I mean, Mom's lake and Audra dying and Chad going into a coma on the same day . . ."

At the mention of Chad's name, Tom paled and stepped away from her. For a second, Zoey worried that Tom was going to close down again — shut her out. But then Tom relaxed.

"What are the chances?" he said grimly.

Zoey stepped toward her brother. "It's not your fault." She touched his arm. "You have to know that."

Tom looked Zoey in the eye. "I don't," he said.

Zoey sighed. She wished there was some way she could take the weight off her brother's shoulders. But he was the only one with the power to lift that burden.

"Just so you know, everything's a mess at school. There are reporters outside the school gates, and Kelly is treating the scene like a red carpet, sobbing about Chad and saying that she and Audra were friends!"

Tom's face shifted again at the mention of Kelly's name. "She did?" he asked, flinching.

Zoey nodded but didn't go on. She knew Tom had it bad for Kelly. So she changed the subject to one they could agree on.

"And hey, word to the wise," she said. "If I were you I'd keep your head down around here. The last thing you need is Dad back on your case."

Tom let out a long sigh. "Be the good son," he said, sounding resigned. "I know I only make things worse by fighting with Dad," he admitted. "But he makes me insane. And when I found the . . ." Tom stopped himself.

"Found what?" Zoey prodded. Tom just shook his head. Zoey could tell that Tom was holding back about something big, but she didn't want to push him back into his shell of fury.

"Thanks for talking to me," she said, giving Tom a hug. Her brother squeezed back.

"Ew." She wrinkled her nose. "Go take a shower," she quipped. She stepped around him and pushed him into the bathroom.

She would have to find out what he was still hiding some other time.

Chapter Ten

Alison wrapped her long Tahari coat around her slender frame and cinched the belt. As she walked up to the towering hospital, she wished the coat could protect her from more than the chill in the air. She wished it could protect her from the sadness, too. Grandmother Diamond had discouraged her from spending her day at the hospital, waiting for Chad to wake up. But Alison had to come, had to be near him.

Stepping into the five-story hospital, Alison made her way down the sterile hall toward the ICU, and hoped she'd be allowed to see him.

"Chad Simon, please," she said to the nurse behind the desk.

"Oh, he's not here anymore," the male nurse said, looking at a computer screen. "They moved him a couple of hours ago."

Alison's heart skipped a beat. "Is he — where did they move him?"

"He's in room three-oh-eight. Third floor." The nurse pointed toward the elevator bank across the hall. Catching Alison's hopeful expression, he added, "He's still under observation." Then in a softer voice he said, "He's still unconscious."

"Right." Alison's heart sank. "Right."

"But the good news is that now he can have regular visitors."

"Thanks." Alison forced a smile before turning toward the elevators and pushing the call button. It wasn't much of a bright side.

A moment later, Alison was standing in front of room 308. Before pushing open the door, she took a deep breath.

The room was larger than the ICU room had been. Lying perfectly still on the bed in the middle of the room, Chad looked as pale as he had two days before — maybe even paler surrounded by the brightly colored flowers sent by well-wishers. There was a window on one side and several chairs for visitors circling the bed. One of them was already filled. Even from the back, Alison could tell Tom wasn't doing so great. His head was down and his shoulders were slumped.

"Hey," Alison said softly, sliding into the chair next to Tom's. "Any news?"

Tom shook his head. "Nope," he said. "Plenty of tests, but no changes."

Reaching out, Alison touched Tom's arm. "It's not your fault," she said.

Tom looked up sharply. She had touched a nerve. "Then whose fault is it?" he asked.

"Nobody's," Alison replied, trying to sound convincing.

"If only I hadn't pushed him . . ." Tom said.

"Didn't Chad come after *you*?" Alison asked gently.

Tom nodded. "He did, but he had a reason to. A friend doesn't —"

"Friendship is complicated," Alison interrupted. "You think you know somebody . . ." She looked at Chad lying motionless in the hospital bed. "But they still have secrets," she finished quietly.

The two of them sat in silence for a while. Alison had been hoping to see Chad alone today, but she was glad Tom was there. It was comforting to be sitting there together.

"Are you going to Audra's funeral tomorrow?" Tom asked suddenly.

Alison shook her head, standing up to brush the curls back from Chad's face. "No. We weren't friends," she explained.

"We weren't really friends, either," Tom said. "I mean, she was just . . . there. . . ." Tom trailed off, his face reddening slightly. "It sounds like I was using her, but I really wasn't." Alison noticed that Tom was talking kind of loudly, as if he urgently needed her to believe him.

"Like I said," Alison offered, "friendship is complicated." She turned to face him. "You know, I think you should go . . . to the funeral. You can say good-bye. Even though you have mixed feelings about Audra, I think it'll make you feel better."

The sound of beeping machines — the ones

monitoring Chad's vital signs — filled the awkward silence that followed. *I shouldn't have said anything*, Alison thought. *He didn't ask for advice — and it's none of my business.*

Slowly, though, Tom began to nod. "Maybe . . ." he said. "Maybe it will make me feel better. One thing's for sure — I definitely couldn't feel much worse."

Chapter Eleven

Alison sat at the giant mahogany table in the formal dining room at Grandmother Diamond's estate — the house Alison currently called home. She stared down at one ornately carved table leg and resisted the urge to kick it. Kicking Tamara Diamond's table would do Alison no more good than kicking Tamara herself — Alison would only be hurting herself in the end. The family matriarch kept not only Alison and the rest of the Diamond clan firmly under her bejeweled thumb, she also owned and controlled nearly everyone in Silver Spring. Grandmother Diamond was the reason Alison's mother — Tamara's own daughter — was currently in jail. But she was also Alison's most powerful ally, and being her grandmother's favorite carried definite benefits . . . most of the time.

Alison took a bite of lamb with mint jelly and chewed slowly. She had no appetite. Her stomach ached from too many cups of hospital coffee two days in a row. And to add insult to injury, Kelly was sitting directly across from her, looking fabulous in a Dolce & Gabbana red crochet sweater and black wool gauchos. Apparently Kelly had seen fit to cap off a full day of shopping by inviting herself to dinner so she could show off the mountain of loot. So much for her caring, concerned girlfriend act. There had to be at least fifteen shopping bags piled in the foyer. And Alison knew the bags were all there just to let her know how much fun Kelly had been having while she'd sat by Chad's bedside — why else would Kelly have made the driver take them out of the car? She and Alison certainly weren't going to be having a "fashion show" the way they used to after a day of retail therapy.

Forget the carved table leg. Alison wished she could kick the size-two tanned leg across from her. It was about as human as mahogany.

"I'm not pleased you girls are getting wrapped up in this coma business," Grandmother Diamond announced from her thronelike chair at the head of the table. She fixed her icy blue eyes on each of them in turn. "I never did like that boy," she murmured.

Alison coughed into her perfectly pressed linen napkin while Francesca, the cook, cleared her plate. Her grandmother had no idea how "wrapped up" she really was. Even lying comatose in a hospital bed all the way across town, Chad had her heart entwined in his.

"And really, Kelly — talking to reporters?" Grandmother Diamond continued. "As if this family isn't in the papers enough already."

Across the table, Kelly practically giggled. Alison glared at her cousin. How could she act so carefree with Chad's life hanging by a thread?

"Grandmother, he *is* my boyfriend," Kelly said sweetly. "And I can't help it if all the newspapers want to talk to me. This is nothing like Aunt Helen's public mess. It's actually quite amazing how supportive everyone is being," she cooed, tilting her head innocently.

Alison tried to let Kelly's little speech roll right off her back. She knew all too well that it was entirely for her benefit, including the dig about her mother. But not letting her cousin's words get under her skin was even harder than eating dinner with a stomachache.

"All I did was casually mention how shopping is my only solace during this horrible wait, and gift certificates started to arrive on my doorstep!" Kelly's voice rose excitedly.

"Diamonds do not accept charity!" Tamara hissed through tight lips, glaring at Kelly. Alison smirked. The fact that Grandmother Diamond saw through Kelly's charade made her feel just the tiniest bit better.

"It's not charity, Grandmother. They are gifts," Kelly defended.

"Don't act smug with me, young lady," Tamara said. Her voice dropped so low that Alison felt chills, even though the iciness was aimed squarely at Kelly. "I can see right through you. I wasn't just talking about the boy, either. Who told the papers that you were close with

Audra Wilson? That simply isn't true. But you just *have* to be in the middle of everything, don't you? Really, Kelly, you're no better than your Aunt Christine."

Grandmother Diamond drew out the last two words carefully, and Alison smiled. Until recently, Kelly'd had no idea that their camera-hungry actress aunt was really Kelly's mother. She had handed her baby girl over to her sister Phoebe to raise and never looked back. The topic was still a bit of a sore spot for Kelly, who wasn't accustomed to being unwanted.

Alison had no idea how her grandmother knew that Kelly and Audra hadn't been friends. Since when did she keep track of the Stafford Academy social scene? It just went to show, Alison figured — Grandmother Diamond was mixed up in *everything*.

Kelly set her napkin down and sniffed. "There's no need to be cruel, Grandmother," she said, pretending to be hurt.

Tamara eyed her dismissively. "You may be excused, Kelly. Fernando can take you home." She turned to her right. "Alison, please remain. I would like a word with you."

Kelly flashed Alison a mischievous look. Alison half expected her to stick out her tongue or break into a taunting chorus of "nyah nyahs." But she just flipped her hair, and left the room. The moment she was out of sight, Grandmother Diamond spoke again.

"At times like this, we must count even the smallest blessings," she said. "At least the tragedies at Stafford are keeping your mother off the front page temporarily. But we may expect a veritable media storm when the trial begins next week."

Alison sensed that her grandmother was waiting for Alison to say something, but had no idea what was expected of her. After several moments of silence, Tamara cleared her throat and looked Alison in the eye.

"This trial is not going to be easy for any of us, but it may be especially hard on you," she said, surprising Alison with her concern. "Have you prepared yourself?"

How? Alison wondered. How could she prepare for something she had no control over? "Yes, Grandmother," she lied, hoping that would be the end of it.

"You know you can talk to me . . . about anything," Grandmother Diamond added.

Alison nodded, finally understanding what her grandmother was getting at. Tamara had just taken Kelly down a notch for *her* benefit. It was a show of solidarity, a little reminder that her grandmother was on her side. What Tamara wanted now was assurance that Alison's allegiance to her was also firm. She wanted a promise that Alison would keep to herself the documents she had found in her grandmother's safe — the ones that proved Tamara was involved in Alison's mother's arrest.

Alison took a sip of water. She had not entirely decided what to do with the papers she'd found. So far, she had done nothing — which was as good as following Grandmother Diamond's orders. So far granddaughter and grandmother were still allies.

"Thank you, Grandmother," Alison said carefully, setting down her crystal water glass. "I think you know how much that means to me."

Grandmother Diamond nodded back. Message received.

Chapter Twelve

Tom stood stiffly in a black Brioni cashmere suit and tie in the chapel parking lot, staring at the peaked double doors and wishing he had never come. What the heck was he doing there?

Leaving, he told himself. *I'm leaving.* He was just turning around when a man and woman dressed in black came out of the double doors and spotted him.

"Tom," the woman called out. Tom walked toward the couple on autopilot. The spectacled woman reached a shaky arm out to him. "We're so glad you're here." It was then that Tom noticed her dark brown eyes. It had to be Audra's mother.

"It means a lot to us," Audra's father said. Except for his dazed expression, he looked just like his daughter had. "It would have meant a lot to Audra."

Tom stared at him. This man had known his mother. She'd trusted him. She had spent countless hours in his office before she died, telling him her deepest secrets, her most private thoughts. Tom stared at the man who had been his mother's psychiatrist and felt suddenly, intensely jealous. How much did he know about the way Tom's mother had died?

"We know how close you and Audra were," Audra's mother said, jolting Tom back to the present. "You must be so lost without her."

Tom nodded numbly, trying to refocus on the current loss. "Yes," he agreed. What else could he say? That he didn't really miss her at all? That she was a lot more like a stalker than a friend?

"We'd like you to say a few words," Audra's father said, putting a hand on Tom's shoulder and looking into his eyes. "At the service."

Audra's mother was nodding emphatically, looking up at him. "Yes, please," she begged.

"Uh . . ." Tom looked from Audra's mother to her father, and back to her mother. Their daughter had just died. They were both grief-stricken. Tom knew what that was like, and that he could not say no. He would do whatever he could to help lessen their pain.

"All right," he agreed, wondering what on earth he was going to say about her.

"Oh, thank goodness," Audra's mother breathed, leading him inside the chapel. "I knew you would want to. It would have meant so much to her. You know, Audra was very, very attached to you."

As Tom stepped inside the second set of doors he felt ill for the hundredth time in three days. That had been exactly the problem with Audra. And just look where it had landed her.

Audra's mother started to lead Tom toward the front row of the crowded chapel, but Tom gently pulled away. "I'll just stand back here," he whispered.

She nodded and walked up the aisle with her husband. Tom leaned against the wall as the minister stepped up to the lectern.

"We are here this afternoon to celebrate the short but meaningful life of Audra Ariel Wilson. . . ." Tom heard Audra's mom let out a little wail, and watched her father put a consoling arm around her shoulder.

Tom tried to focus, to listen to what the minister was saying. It was so odd, he realized, to be tuning out a minister for the second time in a month. His family did not attend services except for PR reasons. His father and Deirdre's wedding had been a disaster . . . but this was much worse. Audra was dead. Gone. For the past few weeks she'd been a constant presence in his life. Now he would never see her again.

Tom shook off those thoughts and looked around the room. The pews were filled. Along with Audra's friends from the debate team and the chess club there were tons more students and teachers, too. It looked like most of the school was there. Many of them were wearing black armbands, and more than a few were crying. The casket in the front was closed and covered in flowers. Wreaths on stands flanked the long box like floral sentries. The minister waved his arms as he spoke about Audra's achievements and passions. Tom braced himself. He knew that in about two minutes, he would be the one up there at the lectern talking about Audra. He rubbed his eyes. *What'd I get myself into?*

"And now Tom Ramirez, Audra's chemistry lab partner and closest friend, will say a few words." Tom's head shot up at the sound of his name. It was time.

Feeling numb, Tom walked up to the podium. He knew he should have something good to say, something meaningful. But he had nothing. Nothing about his relationship with Audra was normal, or easy to put into words.

Tom stared out at the crowded chapel as he waited for the right words to come to him. He spotted X, the mysterious new girl, dressed in an all-black school uniform and sitting in one of the rear pews. Man, that girl was everywhere. It was so weird the way she seemed to be in the middle of everything, yet floated above it all.

Tom blinked. Two rows in front of X was Alison. Yesterday she'd told him she wasn't coming, but here she was. Her smile was bittersweet, her expression encouraging. Tom was grateful to see her face even as he wondered why she had come. And remembering the way Alison listened to him, he remembered Audra's best quality, too.

Drawing comfort from Alison's presence, Tom took a breath and began to speak. "Audra was a true original," he said. "She was unlike anybody else I've ever known."

Thank God, he added to himself as he squared his shoulders and continued.

Chapter Thirteen

Kelly arranged her tousled hair in front of the mirror in the girls' room at Stafford and smiled to herself. Her "back from the beach" piece-y waves looked good. Life was good, too. As it turned out, Chad Simon was a much better boyfriend lying comatose in a hospital bed than he was dragging around on her arm, no matter how great he'd looked there. Unconscious, he was totally no-maintenance, which gave Kelly plenty of time for R & R and shopping. The week-end had been one long retail retreat. And, thanks to Chad, even Monday was feeling luxurious. Having everyone feeling sorry for her provided excellent fringe benefits. All she had to do to get out of class or homework was get a tiny bit misty-eyed and . . . bingo! Free pass.

Who knew playing the victim could get you so far? Kelly mused as she applied a little Benefit blush to her cheeks. Well, maybe Alison did. But pity parties just made her cousin look pathetic.

Kelly selected a waterproof mascara from her Louis Vuitton makeup bag. You never knew when you were going to have to break down in tears. . . .

Her face finished, Kelly adjusted her latest and greatest fashion accessory, the apricot ribbon. It was hard to believe, but she'd gotten the idea from the geeks on the debate team. They'd all started wearing black armbands "in remembrance" of Audra. The armbands were hopelessly dull and unoriginal, but they had sparked an idea in Kelly's brilliant mind.

Just then the door opened and Ruby Sullivan came into the bathroom. "Oh, I just love the ribbons for Chad," she squealed, sidling up to Kelly. "They are sooo fabulous, Kelly. Really. I mean, the whole school is talking about them — everyone wants one." She paused, looking admiringly at the little twisted ribbon pinned to Kelly's See by Chloe blouse. "I really think seeing them is giving the whole school hope."

Kelly smiled at Ruby. She wasn't the richest or prettiest of Kelly's minions, but she did have one good quality — unabashed admiration and devotion. "Aren't they perfect?" Kelly said. "I wanted to wear something that shows I'm thinking of him at every moment."

"Um, can I have one?" Ruby asked meekly. "I want Chad to feel like I'm really thinking about him, too."

"Of course," Kelly said sweetly. She pulled out a sparkly coin purse that she'd filled with perfectly pinned ribbons. Or, rather, had her mother fill with perfectly pinned ribbons.

As Ruby's eyes went wide, Kelly stepped forward and pinned the ribbon onto Ruby's shirt — the exact same black, bell-sleeved Betsey Johnson top Kelly had worn last week. Of course, the shirt had looked much better on Kelly. But she'd already retired it to the back of her closet, anyway.

"Oh, thank you!" Ruby breathed. "I just know he's going to wake up soon."

Kelly nodded. Secretly she hoped that Ruby

was wrong — if Chad recovered too soon, it would ruin all her fun. But she gave Ruby her best sad, brave puppy-dog look before turning back to the mirror to check her reflection one last time. Near perfect, as usual.

While Ruby started blathering on about her new Bourjois lip gloss, Kelly let her thoughts drift to bedside visits. She hadn't been back to the hospital since that first dull night, but she knew she had to stop in eventually, if only to keep Alison's visits from feeling too cozy. The fact that her cousin spent so much time with her boyfriend was getting irritating. If Kelly didn't do something about it, word might get out that her whimpering cousin was always there — waiting, watching, hoping. It was pathetic. Did Alison really think Chad was going to wake up and they'd live happily ever after? What was this, a fairy tale? Kelly smirked. She didn't allow happy endings.

Kelly smoothed her new asymmetric stretch skirt on her way out the door, glad she had a few more hours to feature it at school. It really was a shame to waste this outfit on Mr. Comatose. But then there was always the chance that someone else in room 308 would notice it — someone older and more intriguing. Someone named Dustin. And he would certainly want an apricot ribbon. Kelly grinned. She could even pin it on him herself. . . .

Chapter Fourteen

Alison sat on a polished bench in the federal courthouse. After all the waiting and anticipation, her mother's trial was finally starting. Quickly, Alison stole a glance at the clock on the wall. 10:10. She and her grandmother had arrived promptly at nine (Tamara was never late). Alison's butt was already numb when the prosecutor in a pinstriped suit began making his opening statement. Shaking his head, he began telling the court how Helen Rose had stolen money from company shareholders and used it for her own gain. How she lied to the government about her profits and investments so she wouldn't have to pay the taxes she owed.

"Every honest, hardworking, middle-class citizen contributes a portion of their low wages to keep the country running," the prosecutor said. "But Helen Rose, who is worth more than all of her employees *combined*, considered herself exempt. She was raking it in and cheating us all. Ladies and gentlemen of the jury, she *must* be held accountable."

Alison resisted the urge to rush to her mother's defense. From the way the prosecutor presented Helen Rose, she was not only a lawbreaker but also an awful human being. A liar. A cheat. Someone who obviously put herself above others. But even if she had the nerve to defend her mother, what could she say? Quite a bit of it was true . . .

Feeling numb, Alison looked around the courtroom. It was standing room only — jam-packed with spectators and reporters. Her mother's humiliation was so . . . public.

Next to her, Grandmother Diamond reached over and patted Alison's hand. Alison sat up straighter. She looked directly ahead at her mother's ramrod-straight back. What was *she* feeling? Fear? Remorse? Embarrassment? Anger?

And her grandmother. Alison risked a furtive glance at the woman sitting next to her in an exquisitely tailored wool tweed suit and matching gray pearls. As usual, Tamara Diamond's expression gave away nothing.

Reaching just inside her collar, Alison felt the small silver key there — the only thing her father had left for her when he'd disappeared out of the blue a few weeks before. She had no idea what the key opened, if anything. And though she now knew he'd been sent off to rehab in Belize, and that Grandmother Diamond and Aunt Phoebe were wrapped up in it somehow, she still had no idea how to reach him. All she knew was that she wished he were there now with her. Maybe then her choices would be different.

When the prosecutor was finished, Helen's lead defense lawyer got to his feet. Hope surged in Alison's chest as she took in his confident pose. His shoes were highly polished and his salmon-colored tie looked elegant against his ecru shirt. But somehow Alison had a difficult time believing him when he spoke. He claimed that Helen Rose had been framed — that her own employees had plotted against her, that the nature of her career inflamed jealousies and incited spite crimes. That when the evidence was presented, the jury would have no choice but to clear her name.

But, Alison wondered, how could they present evidence that was stashed under Zoey's mattress? She hoped her mother's lawyers had some other form of proof, that the documents she had wouldn't be needed.

Finally the opening statements were finished. The judge declared a recess and Helen Rose got to her feet. Alison caught her mother's eye as the bailiff led her away by the elbow. Helen nodded slightly at her daughter but did not smile. She appeared to avoid her mother's gaze altogether. Alison wondered if her mom was looking at her just so she would not have to look at Grandmother Diamond.

A tightening grip on Alison's arm put a stop to her wondering. "It's time to go," her grandmother said tightly, nudging her forward.

Alison nodded. She suddenly felt like she was suffocating. She wanted desperately to race out of the courtroom, to burst outside and gulp in fresh air. Instead she took a deep breath and ignored her racing heart. "Of course," she said as calmly as she could.

As she and her grandmother made their way out of the courtroom, Alison spotted a familiar face in the crowd — Jeremy Jones — and did a double take. When he saw Alison look his way, Jeremy lifted his hand in greeting, and she waved back, smiling for the first time all day. It was good to see a friendly face.

"Who is that?" Tamara asked sharply, her eyes narrowing on Jeremy.

"Zoey's tutor," Alison replied.

"What is he doing here?" Tamara asked. She sounded tense.

Alison shrugged. *Good question.*

Outside, Tamara and Alison were bombarded by reporters, who shot rapid-fire questions at the two of them. Alison ignored them — and was stunned that her grandmother did not.

"Mrs. Diamond, are you here in support of your daughter?" a man in an overcoat asked.

Tamara raised her chin. "I am here for my family," she said curtly.

"Have you and Helen made amends?" another reporter prodded.

Grandmother Diamond didn't hesitate. "There is no bridge that cannot be rebuilt," she replied, easily dodging the question.

A deluge of inquiries followed, but Tamara shook them off. "I have to think of my granddaughter now," she said. "It's been a long and exhausting morning for her. Now if you'll excuse us, we'd like to get some lunch."

Ha, Alison thought. Food was the last thing she wanted. But she was glad to get away from the throng. The shouting and the flashing cameras made her head hurt.

Safe inside the limo and pulling away from the courthouse, Alison felt her breathing return to normal.

"The pageantry is quite offensive," Tamara complained as the car merged into a lane of traffic.

Alison didn't reply. Despite her grandmother's words, she could see the older woman smiling to herself. This was, as usual, her carefully created production.

"Could you have Fernando drop me at the hospital, please?" Alison asked. "I'd like to visit Chad."

Tamara snorted. "I don't understand why you are so concerned about that boy, Alison. He'll either pull out of the coma or he won't, and exhausting yourself over him will accomplish nothing. You would do well to follow your cousin's lead on this matter. You don't see her running herself ragged over him, now do you? And I don't see what more he has to offer you."

"I just want to be with him," Alison said quietly. She did not expect her grandmother to understand about love. She braced herself for further objection, but none came.

"Please stop at the hospital, Fernando," Tamara said, and the matter was dropped.

Ten minutes later, Alison was walking down the hall on her way to Chad's room. It felt comforting to be in the relative quiet of the hospital, away from the crowds and drama outside the trial. In a way, she was grateful for the distraction Chad's illness provided.

Wait, did you just admit you're glad *the guy you love is in a coma?* Alison scolded herself. *How warped are you?*

Alison reached for the handle on Chad's door, but it began to turn before she touched

89

it. Someone was coming out. Alison drew in her breath sharply, surprised at the hopeful feeling flitting in her chest like a trapped butter-fly. *Tom?*

Stupid. Alison chastised herself as one of the nurses came out of Chad's room, smiling. She felt her cheeks glowing in embarrassment. *You came to see Chad, remember?*

Chapter Fifteen

Kelly strode into the front entrance of Silver Spring General Hospital like a model on the runway, enjoying the feeling of her hair blowing around her neck. She really did look good today.

The elevator arrived just as she reached for the button — yet another example of her magic touch — and she got on ahead of three other visitors and a pair of nurses. While the elevator made its way to the third floor, she listened in on the nurses' hospital gossip.

"Any change with the boy in the coma?" the male nurse asked.

The other nurse shook her head. "None. They're getting ready to do another EKG."

The guy nodded. "Poor kid. He's so young. I hope he wakes up."

"Me, too," the other nurse agreed. "Have you seen his girlfriend?"

"Yes, poor thing — talk about devoted."

Kelly beamed as the nurses went on about how wonderful she was. She'd never really been into nurses — they wore such hideous ortho-pedic white shoes . . . blech. But these two were obviously perceptive.

"She's here almost every day," the female nurse said.

Kelly's jaw dropped. They weren't talking about her, they were talking about Alison! Scowl-ing, Kelly stamped her foot. The two nurses briefly turned in her direction, then got back to their conversation just as the elevator doors opened.

Kelly glowered all the way to Chad's room. How could they think that Alison's display of devotion was anything but pathetic? It was dis-gusting! And she was *not* Chad's girlfriend.

Shoving open the door and storming inside,

Kelly gave Alison an extra-nasty look and planted herself between her cousin's bedside seat — *her* seat — and Chad.

"Don't you ever go home?" Kelly snarled. Then she smiled. "Oh, right. You don't have a home."

Kelly was trying to think of something else to say when the perfect subject popped into her mind. How could she have forgotten what day this was? "How was the trial?" she asked snidely.

Alison gazed at her steadily and said nothing. Instead she stood up and squeezed Chad's hand in a (barf) silent good-bye. Like he could feel it.

Kelly glanced over at Chad, who looked as pasty and lifeless as ever. She really didn't want to be left alone with the vegetable, and she wasn't going to leave until Dustin had seen her, so she kept talking.

"It really is good of you to stay with Chad," she said sweetly. "Especially since Will can't be here." Kelly silently tapped her boot toe on the floor, waiting for Alison to react.

"Who's Will?" Alison asked, turning around. *Good girl.*

"Wait. Are you telling me that Chad never told you about *Will*?" Kelly said, looking appropriately aghast. "They are so close! I just assumed you knew all about him. . . ." She paused, looking around the room thoughtfully before she brought her gaze back to Alison. "But then I guess it was that whole trust thing that broke you two up. How sad for you. Chad never could tell you his secrets."

"Who is Will?" Alison repeated tonelessly. She looked as if she didn't believe a word Kelly was saying, which made it all the more rich.

"He's Chad's little brother," Kelly said slowly. "He's autistic, and Chad is practically raising him. He means everything to Chad. It's too bad you haven't met him, actually. Sweet kid."

Kelly watched the expression on Alison's face change from casual disbelief to surprise to horror.

Her own expression changed, too. She couldn't keep from smiling. Who said hospital visits couldn't be fun?

Chapter Sixteen

Tom rolled over for the hundredth time, kicking the covers off his body. He needed to sleep. Badly. But whenever he closed his eyes, the image of Chad lying on the floor at his feet came speeding into his brain like an out-of-control car. The image slammed into Tom, sending him reeling. Crumpled at his feet, Chad looked weak, confused . . . afraid. His eyes were pleading. No way could Tom sleep through that.

Tom sat up and took a drink of water, trying to shake the image from his head. He'd known that something weird was going on with Chad. Chad had told him that he'd been having head- aches and wasn't feeling too great. But Tom had

thought Chad was just making up excuses —
reasons to copy Tom's homework, reasons
beyond the fact that his girlfriend, Kelly, took up
a lot of time.

Only now did Tom see they weren't excuses.
How could he have ignored the fact that Chad
had been losing so much weight? How could he
have written off Chad's dizzy spells?

Why didn't I ask him about it? Tom quizzed
himself. *Why? Why? Why?*

Because I was too busy going after Kelly, he
told himself miserably. He was so busy looking
at his best friend's girl that he didn't see what
was going on with his best friend. And now that
Chad was in a coma? Tom still wanted to be
with Kelly.

Tom shook his head. No. He didn't. He
couldn't. He had to be true to Chad. He wanted
to be a good friend again, more than anything.
But Kelly was just so . . . so . . .

Ugh. He was *sick.* Tom adjusted his pillow
and lay back down.

When he closed his eyes this time, it was
Kelly's face he saw, her hair, her eyes, her smile.
Who could resist them? And then, suddenly,

she was there sitting next to him. His room was gone. They were in a car together, out for a drive. Kelly was behind the wheel. The top was down. The wind was blowing her golden hair all around her face, and she was laughing at one of his jokes.

In the next moment they were out of the car, standing by some water. The lake at Great Falls! They were at the lake. Tom wanted to show Kelly something. They walked up the path together, to the spot Audra had brought him to. When the path widened into an overhang Kelly reached for Tom's hand, squeezing it tight as he pulled her farther out.

The spray from the waterfall dampened Kelly's face, making her skin glisten and her eyelashes clump together. She was so beautiful.

Kelly danced a few steps, enjoying the refreshing spray. Then she rushed up to Tom, her arms open for a hug. Tom held her for a long moment, his heart racing. But when he pulled back to look at Kelly's face, it had changed. He wasn't holding Kelly, he was holding Audra!

Confused, Tom pushed the girl away. Audra screamed in horror and anger as she fell back.

Tom reached out a hand. Too late. Audra plummeted over the edge of the cliff.

With his mouth open in a silent scream, Tom peered over the ledge, helpless. The figure lying at the bottom of the drop, caught in the rocks, was twisted. Her hair splayed out. Her arms impossibly bent. Her face . . .

Tom opened his mouth wider. He tried to scream again and again, straining until the pain in his chest was unbearable, but no sound came out.

The face on the figure was not Kelly's, or Audra's. It was his mother's.

"Mom!" Tom pushed the scream out into the wind and spray. "Mom!"

Drenched in sweat, Tom sat up in bed. His heart was beating so hard he thought it might burst out of his chest. Had he yelled out loud?

Tom looked around his room, waiting to feel comforted by the knowledge that it was all a dream. He never did.

Chapter Seventeen

Zoey stepped out of the bathroom stall and smiled at the girl standing in front of the mirror. "Hey," she said, hanging her messenger-bag strap on the corner of the sink. Before Zoey could even turn on the water, the wide-eyed freshman raced out the door with dripping-wet hands.

"Have a nice day," Zoey called after her with fake cheerfulness. Her reputation had been borderline scary before — now with the Audra rumors and the horrible somber mood at school, it was out of control. Still, she couldn't believe that people were actually afraid of her.

How crazy was that? She should have just shouted "Boo!"

Squinting at her reflection, Zoey turned her face from side to side. Okay, so it was not her best hair day. Her dark razor cut was messier than it should be. Her long blond-streaked bangs needed a trim and she could use some fresh highlights. But she didn't think she looked frightening. A little different, maybe. A touch too much eyeliner, maybe. But not scary. Unless you already believed that she was a cold-blooded killer.

Shutting off the water with a sigh, Zoey grabbed a paper towel. It was getting hard to maintain a sense of humor. The whole "Zoey killed Audra" thing was not dying down like regular school gossip. Every morning there was new graffiti on her locker. (The janitors were probably loving her for that.) Every afternoon there were whispers and snickers in the hall. And now some freaked-out freshman was afraid to be in the same room with her!

Shouldering her bag, Zoey headed for history, her favorite class. Even though she hadn't been going to her tutoring sessions, she was still pulling straight As across the board. Only now that Audra was gone, being at the head of the class left a bitter taste in her mouth.

Zoey rounded a corner and spotted one of the few people at school who still treated her like a human being — her brother.

"Hey," she greeted him. He did not look right. "You okay?"

Tom glanced down at her blankly, his eyes ringed in dark circles. His clothes looked like he had put them on straight off the bedroom floor.

Zoey dropped her voice and changed direction, steering Tom down the hall with her. She had planned to talk to Tom about this later, but . . . "I've been hearing you at night," she said quietly. "I'm worried."

Tom blinked several times. His face twitched.

"It's all right, Tom," Zoey said softly. "It's just me."

Tom wiped his face with his sleeve, then shook his head. "It's just nightmares. Look, I've got to go," he said, avoiding her gaze. "I'll catch you later, Zo," he said. And then he was gone.

Zoey felt her heart sink. She knew school wasn't the ideal place for gut spilling, but she felt like Tom was slipping away again. And right now she needed him more than ever.

Chapter Eighteen

Zoey fidgeted as the cab stopped at yet another red light on Colesville Road as it made its way from Stafford Academy through the revitalized downtown of Silver Spring, toward Hardwired. It might have been nice to linger around the old deco buildings, spruced up theater, and silver diner — take in the scene and the fall colors — *if* Zoey was a tourist in town for DC business. But Zoey was no tourist. All she wanted to do was get across town so she could see Jeremy.

Zoey hadn't had a single tutoring session since Audra had died. Jeremy had called her as soon as he heard the news about Chad and Audra, but Zoey'd told him that she needed some time to regroup, and he hadn't pressed. The truth was, she was afraid things would be weird with Jeremy. She knew he would believe her if she told him what happened, she just didn't want to have to explain things. And if he *did* see her differently, Zoey didn't want to face that. Besides Alison, Jeremy was the only person in Silver Spring Zoey felt truly connected to. She practically lived for their time together — and not just because he was gorgeous. Jeremy was also a stellar listener.

After avoiding him for almost a week, Zoey was suffering from serious withdrawal. She needed a dimple fix. So she'd told Jeremy she'd meet him at Hardwired right after school. Which was now.

When the cab finally pulled up outside the coffee shop, Zoey threw the driver a twenty and jumped out, not even bothering to wait for her change. Now that she was so close to seeing Jeremy again, she couldn't imagine why she had waited this long. Peering through the glass door as she pulled it open, Zoey spotted him. He was waiting at their regular table with a macchiato for himself and a latte for her. Zoey took a deep breath and approached the table. She was ready to tell him everything.

"Hey," she said as she slid into the chair across from him.

"Hey," he greeted. "I've missed you."

Zoey brushed her bangs out of her eyes. "It's been a little crazy," she said. The world's largest understatement.

Jeremy nodded. "No kidding. I can't believe how everyone's blowing this out of proportion."

Zoey felt hot tears waiting in the wings. If she could just keep from crying, everything would be okay. Jeremy seemed ready as ever to listen.

"I mean, they're totally out to get her. It's disgusting," Jeremy blurted.

What? Who? Zoey shook her head, confused. "Who's out to get who?" she asked.

Jeremy sat back in his chair. "Helen Rose, of course," he said, as if it were obvious. "I just have one question: What happened to 'innocent until proven guilty'?" He threw up his hands. Zoey had never seen him look so frustrated, or act so clueless.

She stared across the table at her tutor. Part of her was relieved that he wasn't grilling her about why she hadn't shown up at their sessions for a week or what she'd been going through since she watched Audra die. But another part of her desperately wanted him to hear what she had to say. Why couldn't he stop obsessing about Helen Rose long enough to think about anyone else — like maybe her?!

"I just can't get over the stuff the media is doing to her family — it'll be a miracle if they can ever live a normal life again after this."

"Yeah, right," Zoey muttered halfheartedly. As if anyone in Alison's family had *ever* lived a "normal life." But what did Jeremy care? He wasn't Alison Rose's best friend, Zoey was.

Zoey pulled out a book, desperate to change the subject. Could she actually pretend she didn't understand her math homework so they could talk about something else? Lame-o. But desperate times called for desperate measures.

"You know, I hate to change the subject, but I really need your help with this math," Zoey murmured, opening to a random page. "I can't really think about anything else." She looked up at Jeremy just as a familiar and not particularly welcome face walked through the door behind him, carrying several shopping bags.

What was Kelly Reeves doing at Hardwired?

Chapter Nineteen

Caffeine. Caffeine was what Kelly needed. All this shopping was starting to wear her out. But when Kelly had told her mom at breakfast how exhausted she was from worrying about Chad (an excuse for getting out of going to see her mom's shrink after school), Phoebe had suggested she buy herself something pretty to cheer herself up and take her mind off it instead. Of course Kelly had agreed. After all, who was she to refuse?

Kelly stood impatiently at the back of the line in the small café. The place was cute, with dark wood booths, cozy tables, and even a fireplace. But what was with the service? It was taking forever to just order and she didn't have all the time in the world. Besides, her shopping bags were heavy!

Kelly set her bags down and tapped her foot impatiently. You would think someone would recognize her and call her to the front of the line. Uh, hello? Didn't these people know her boyfriend was in a coma? Didn't they notice her apricot ribbon?

Kelly glared at the back of the woman in front of her, willing her to order or get out of the way. The woman just stood there staring at the coffee menu like an idiot, so Kelly looked for a distraction in the rest of the room. The usual café crowd was there, losers with laptops, bookworms, and a few couples holding hands and blowing on their steamy drinks. Yawn.

Choke. Kelly's eyes alighted on a couple bent over a book. They had their heads together and the girl looked terribly familiar. There was no way Kelly could miss the bad eye-makeup job on Zoey Ramirez. But what held her attention was not the sloppy liner — it was the college hottie Pyro Girl was with. He was criminally cute. So what was he doing with Zoey?

"How can I help you?" Of course as soon as she was distracted the line had moved. A spotty-faced guy behind the counter was smiling hugely at Kelly, waiting to take her order. "What'll it be?"

"Nonfat, large double latte," Kelly said, without returning the pockmarked boy's silly smile. She had other things on her mind. The plan she'd been cooking up to keep herself occupied while Chad was unconscious was starting to sound even sweeter.

If Zoey Ramirez could hook a college boy, it would be a piece of cake for Kelly. And the one she had in mind would make the perfect accessory to her autumn wardrobe: Dustin Simon.

Kelly's mind whirred while she waited for her latte. *Come on, come on!* she thought. For all she knew, family visiting hours were happening at Silver Spring General right now, and there was a shoulder in Chad's room that she *really* wanted to cry on. She still felt weak-kneed from the smile he'd given her the last time she was at the hospital, when he'd accepted her apricot ribbon. She didn't have time to wait around for some slow kid to pull her double shots.

Finally the clerk set the paper cup down on the counter. Kelly grabbed it and rushed out the door. There was no time to waste. If she played her cards right, Kelly could move seamlessly from one Simon brother to the next. And Kelly always played her cards right.

Tonio pulled the family SUV up in front of the café and loaded Kelly's bags. "Hospital, T," Kelly told him, sliding into the back. Kelly thought she saw the driver's eyebrows go up, but he knew better than to say anything. All the way to the hospital Kelly watched scenes between herself and Dustin in her head. It was a good thing Chad was in a coma and not just sick in bed, because she was pretty sure he'd be totally jealous. But really, who could blame her for upgrading to the older brother? Anyone with any sense would do the same thing. . . .

Kelly stepped off the elevator (nurse-free, thank goodness) and waltzed down the hall. Opening the door to Chad's room, she donned her best distressed look.

Ugh. Kelly took a sip of her latte to keep from groaning aloud. Dustin was nowhere to be seen. Instead the show being put on at Chad's bedside theater was the same old dreary teary drama that played almost every day and starred Alison and Tom. Ho hum.

The two bleeding hearts were leaning close to each other and talking in hushed tones. When they spotted Kelly they immediately pulled apart and the only audible sounds were the annoying clicks and beeps and whirs of Chad's machinery.

Kelly had interrupted something, she realized with a small smile. *Good.*

Slipping her printed Emilio Pucci tote off her shoulder, Kelly dropped it into a chair. "Gang's all here, huh?" She stayed on her feet, looking down her perfect ski-jump nose at her cousin. "Anyone seen Dustin?"

Tom shook his head and stood up. "I'm going for a soda. Can I get you anything?" he asked Alison. Alison shook her head and Kelly bristled as Tom left the room. Sure, she was holding a drink. But he should still offer her one, too. It was the least he could do.

Biting back her annoyance, Kelly scowled at Alison.

"So, Alison," Kelly said. "I just got off the

phone with Grandmother Diamond. She said the trial is going really well and they may be able to get an early conviction. You must be thrilled." Kelly clapped her hands together at the "fantastic" news she was delivering, then added, "Oooh, and we made a spa date for tomorrow." She flounced down into one of the chairs next to Chad's bed. "You're so lucky, living with her and all."

Kelly grinned as she watched Alison's face fall. Goody. Her cousin's little balloon of hope was deflated. It wasn't a totally wasted hospital trip after all.

Chapter Twenty

If she let her head drop back on the leather seat, Alison could look up through the slanted back window of her grandmother's Rolls and watch the brightly colored trees whiz past. Fernando was driving fast and singing loudly along to the stereo, like he usually did when it was just him and Alison. They both knew that if Grandmother Diamond knew about his behavior she would have something to say about it. And they both knew neither of them would ever let on.

The trees and telephone poles were zooming past as quickly as the thoughts racing in Alison's mind. She lingered for only a split second on each subject — Chad's unchanging condition, her long conversations with Tom, Zoey's troubles since Audra's death, her mother's poker face at the trial. But one of her worries kept coming back again and again: Kelly. No matter how she tried, Alison could not manage to shake Kelly out of her head.

When Kelly had first appeared in Chad's room that afternoon Alison had wanted to knock her over. And for once it was not because she had lied — it was because she had told the truth. Ironically, at the very moment Kelly had walked in, Tom had been telling Alison all about Chad's little brother, Will. It turned out there really *was* a Will. He really *was* autistic. And Chad really *did* take care of him —they were very close. And Kelly and Tom really were the only ones who knew about him.

So why hadn't Chad ever told *her* about him? Alison understood why Chad didn't want the word out at Stafford. But did he think he had to keep Will a secret from her? The truth was locked in Chad's head. If Alison wanted it, she would just have to wait.

The idea that Chad trusted Kelly more than he trusted her made Alison feel faint. But what really confused her was that, about this at least, Kelly had been *honest*. That little fact threw everything into question. Was she also being honest about chumming around with Grandmother Diamond? Was she telling the truth when she said their grandmother was predicting an early conviction? Both seemed unlikely. And yet . . . it would be just like Her Highness to buy Kelly back into her clutches. Indulgence was the way to Kelly's heart — or, rather, the hole where her heart should be. And it would be just like Kelly to take the bait (and slip the hook).

Thankfully, not long after Kelly showed up, Chad's parents arrived. They looked exhausted, and Alison and Tom had cleared out to give them some room and privacy to visit their son. Kelly, of course, stayed where she was. Before Alison could even get out of the room, Kelly was pinning those ridiculous ribbons on both of the Simons. Alison hoped Chad's parents could see through her game, but knew not many people did.

Dragging her head up off the seat back, Alison stared at the winding, tree-lined road ahead.

They were almost back at the Diamond estate. Now was the time to get to the bottom of at least one Kelly issue.

With a quick thanks to Fernando, Alison stepped out of the car and made her way inside. She was planning to ask her grandmother straight out if she had plans with Kelly for the weekend, and if she really thought her mother was going to get an early conviction.

When she stepped into the screening room, plans changed. Grandmother Diamond was watching TV, her face crinkled into a look of disapproval. Alison stared at the plasma screen and saw what was disturbing her.

Aunt Christine's beautiful face took up all fifty inches. She was being interviewed on one of those "hard-hitting" infotainment shows where the lighting was as soft focus as the questions.

Giving her lazy, confidential smile, Aunt Christine easily tossed back the softball questions. She was probably supposed to be plugging her new movie, but of course the conversation had moved to the topic of her now-infamous oldest sister, Helen Rose.

"Chuck," Aunt Christine said, leaning in

toward the interviewer with a sexy yet earnest look in her green eyes, "honestly, I just can't wait until this is all over. Who cares what the verdict is? I just want my sister back. I've always thought drama was best left on the big screen. Like my character in the new Harris Jones epic —"

Ha! Alison could not believe her ears. Aunt Christine was hardly the supportive sister. Hearing her talk as though she cared one bit about Helen made Alison want to laugh . . . or cry.

"Turn it off!" Grandmother Diamond barked, making Alison jump.

Stepping in front of her grandmother, Alison pressed the POWER button on the set. Tamara sat back in her chair. "I could not have stood that a second more," she growled, putting a hand on her short white hair near her high forehead. "Who does she think she is? Using the trial for personal gain . . . and . . . and . . ." Tamara seemed at a loss for words. She stood up and began to pace, her gold-handled cane thumping on the floor with each stride.

Alison backed up toward the door, wishing she had never come in. Her grandmother was unusually flustered — and worse, furious. But why was she suddenly so upset about one in a long line of Christine-milks-the-press interviews?

Tamara crossed to the fireplace and whirled to face Alison. "What was she thinking?" she snarled. "What could possibly have possessed her to tell Kelly that long-held family secret?"

Alison stared at her grandmother, struggling to keep her face blank. Grandmother Diamond wasn't upset about the interview. She was upset about Christine telling Kelly that she was her real mother.

"Thank goodness Kelly had the good sense to tell me what happened," Tamara said, her voice calming down a bit. "Christine has my drive," she said as she started to pace again. "But she inherited no taste, and quite obviously missed out on judgment as well."

Alison nodded, not wanting her grandmother to stop ranting. This was the most real information she had gotten out of her in a long time. Aunt Christine was seriously in the doghouse.

"The last thing we need is for people to start asking *more* questions." Grandmother Diamond paused and looked over at Alison. "It's her career I worry about," she added.

Yeah, right, Alison thought, still keeping quiet. She had several questions of her own about the family laundry, like: What threat was all this to Aunt Christine's career? And who was Kelly's real father? But she knew better than to ask her grandmother now, so she just smiled tightly.

Grandmother Diamond switched gears. "Alison, you are not to attend the trial any longer. I fear your presence there is not good for you or your mother."

"But . . ." Alison stammered.

"You're a distraction. I see you trying to catch your mother's eye," Tamara said matter-of-factly. She was not discussing, she was informing.

Alison's jaw dropped. She may have tried to look at her mother — read something in her face. But her mother had only glanced at her once, and her expression had registered nothing.

"It's for your own good," Tamara insisted, not acknowledging Alison's distraught look. "You need to focus on your studies. You're already distracted enough by that . . . vegetable."

Vegetable? Did she just call Chad a vegetable?

Alison felt like a bird in a gilded cage — one who had just gotten her wings clipped for good measure. There would be no flying free. Alison folded. "If you think that's best, Grandmother," she conceded quietly.

Hating herself for swallowing every nasty pill her grandmother offered up, Alison backed out of the room. She felt powerless. Behaving as her grandmother wanted her to was the only way she could survive — Her Highness made sure of that. But little by little, Alison was losing everything that mattered.

Chapter Twenty-one

Alison sat across from her grandmother at breakfast on Saturday. Her anger had been simmering for several days and was threatening to boil over. Yes, Grandmother Diamond had been more than generous to Alison since her mother's arrest. But that didn't give her the right to cut her off from her own parents. It was time for Alison to take a stand. "I'm going to see Mother today," she announced as she set her serrated spoon down next to her grapefruit.

Grandmother Diamond did not flinch at the announcement. "That's a good idea. I'm sure she's feeling a bit . . . down," she said calmly. "I think your Aunt Phoebe was planning to visit her today as well. I'll telephone her and the two of you can go together."

Alison grimaced. She had gotten what she wanted — but on Tamara's terms. Her grandmother was sending a chaperone.

Obedient as ever, Phoebe arrived before Alison had brushed her teeth.

"This'll be fun," Aunt Phoebe gushed as Alison climbed into the back of the Reeves' SUV. "A little time with my favorite niece."

"Your only niece," Alison muttered, wishing she could close the car door herself so she could give it a good slam. But that was Tonio's job. Beside her, Aunt Phoebe kept right on yammering about nothing.

After they had signed into the visitors' log at the jail, and gone through the maze of heavy locked doors to the visitors' room, Alison steeled herself and turned to her aunt. "I'd really like to talk to my mother alone," she said with a fake smile.

Phoebe's eyes widened slightly. "Oh, well, I —"

Alison pointed to a chair against the back wall. "I'll only be a few minutes," she said, stepping up to the thick glass separating prisoners from visitors just as a door on the other side opened and her mother appeared. Helen was dressed in an orange jumpsuit, and unlike on trial days, she was not wearing makeup. Clearly, she was not expecting visitors, and she looked neither happy nor sad to see Alison. She just looked drained. She smiled wanly at Alison, then spotted Phoebe but pretended not to. Sitting down on the other side of the table divided by the glass wall, she picked up the phone to speak to her daughter.

"This is a surprise. What is *she* doing here?" Helen asked bluntly.

"Grandmother sent her," Alison replied. She made an instantaneous decision to report all of the bad news ASAP. "I'm sorry I won't be there for the rest of your trial," she added softly.

"What? What are you talking about?" Helen demanded. "I thought the school granted permission. Aren't you keeping up with your schoolwork?"

Alison's eyes narrowed. Of course her mother assumed it was a performance issue. She was always waiting, watching to see if Alison would fail. It was like she didn't believe Alison was capable of maintaining her mother's perfect image. It made Alison feel like a stain. "No!" Alison didn't care if she sounded annoyed. "I mean, yes! I am keeping up, of course. That's not it. Grandmother has forbidden me to attend." Alison watched her mother's eyes change. It was like a cloud moved across them — a storm front.

"Nobody can keep you from going to the trial. It's your choice. She can't *make* you abandon me," Helen said accusingly.

"I didn't choose this, Mom," Alison retorted hotly. She wasn't the one who got arrested and put on trial. She wasn't the one who was estranged from Grandmother Diamond. "With you locked up and Dad gone I have to look after myself however I can."

Alison shivered. Once again she felt pulled between her mother and her grandmother. But every time she spoke with her mother, the choice seemed clearer. The last time Alison had come here, Helen had lied to her point-blank. She'd sat on the other side of the glass and calmly denied that Grandmother Diamond had visited her, even though she knew that not five minutes earlier Alison had seen Tamara leaving the prison.

"Look at me, Alison." Helen put her face close to the bulletproof glass. "I need you on my side."

Sure. I should give you *trust and loyalty and in return* I *get . . .* Alison stared. She had come here thinking she was ready to give her mother another chance. But once again, her mother was only lecturing her and letting her down. So she changed the subject.

"I got a postcard from Dad," she said evenly, tucking a lock of hair behind her ear.

For a split second Helen looked surprised, then quickly leaned back, hiding all signs of interest. Alison could tell she wanted more information. And she would give it to her, but on her terms.

"He's in some rehab in Belize. Whoever shipped him off wanted him *way* out of the way." Remembering the conversation about "cleaning up messes" she'd overheard between her grandmother and Aunt Phoebe after her father disappeared, Alison wondered if she

126

should tell her mother Aunt Phoebe was involved.

She didn't need to. Alison could see the gears in her mother's head turning. Then she noticed Helen looking past her at Phoebe. As usual, Helen had a hunch of her own.

"My sweet sister's doing, no doubt," she said, more to herself than to Alison. "Your Aunt Phoebe might look like a useless puddle of sap, but sometimes she surprises us all. And, of course, she's easily manipulated by Mother."

Alison didn't point out that her dad's need for rehab was real — his drinking had been a big problem for years. She knew full well that Aunt Phoebe hadn't shipped off Jack Rose to help him. She had gotten rid of Jack to hurt Helen.

"I hope you see what they are doing, Alison." Helen tore her glare from her sister and leaned closer to the glass — closer to Alison. "They are trying to make me less human by taking away my husband and now my daughter. They are trying to make it easier for the jury to lock me up like some sort of unfeeling monster. You do *see* that Alison, don't you?" her mom pressed.

Alison nodded numbly before hanging up

the phone. Yes, she saw the portrait the prosecution was painting of an unfeeling, driven career woman bent on fame and success at the cost of her family. The picture was all too familiar. And all too true.

Chapter Twenty-two

"Good morning, sunshine!"

Zoey flinched at the sound of Deirdre's perky chirp and quickly ducked into the pantry cupboard to avoid being enveloped in a fluffy pink hug.

"Mmh," she grunted in reply. Deirdre was a hugger — and she considered Tom and Zoey fair game. You couldn't even get breakfast anymore without watching your back.

Grabbing a cereal bar and a bottle of water, Zoey turned to beat a hasty retreat to her room, but Deirdre was blocking her so she slumped onto a stool at the huge kitchen island.

"You know, Zo Zo, I was thinking . . ." Deirdre burbled, unfazed by Zoey's clear lack of interest, or the face she made at the nickname Deirdre had invented. It made Zoey sound like a trained monkey. "We haven't bonded in ages. How about a shopping day? Just us girls!"

How about not? Zoey thought, nearly choking. Hanging with Deirdre was not what she had in mind for her Saturday. She was thinking more along the lines of downloading some new music, catching a matinee with Alison, and eating herself sick on movie popcorn.

"No, thanks." Zoey flashed a fake smile. "I —"

"I think a girls' day sounds like a great idea," DA Daddy interrupted, sweeping into the room and accepting Deirdre's bouncy embrace. Where had he come from?

Zoey's head snapped up and she glared at her dad. He was already dressed in a suit and tie — another lazy weekend day for him . . . at the office. He probably thought a girls' day sounded like a good idea because it would get him off the hook with his neglected wife. But Zoey was not Deirdre's babysitter. Ignoring

Deirdre's happy clapping and excited squeals, Zoey shot her dad an angry look.

"I have plans," she said firmly.

"Change them," the DA shot back.

"I have tutoring," Zoey tried again. She didn't actually have an appointment with Jeremy but she was hoping schoolwork would hold a little bit more weight with her father.

"If your tutor can't be flexible, I'll find you a new one," her dad threatened.

"Fine." Zoey gave in. It was the longest conversation she'd had with her father in more than a week — and already she missed the silent treatment.

Chapter Twenty-three

Aunt Phoebe and Alison were halfway home before Phoebe started in with the chatter. "Are you okay, honey?" she cooed.

"Fine. Head hurts, that's all." Alison closed her eyes, hoping to end the conversation.

"It must be so hard to see your mom like that. All locked up. You must miss her." Aunt Phoebe put on a sickening baby voice that made Alison's skin crawl. It was clear she wasn't going to shut up, so Alison gave in and opened her eyes. If her aunt wanted to talk, fine. They'd talk.

"If I miss her too much I can always pick up a newspaper," Alison said dismissively. "What I really want is to talk to my dad."

Aunt Phoebe kept nodding with her face all screwed up in a "poor thing" pout.

"So, do you think you can help me contact him?" Alison pushed.

Guilt flickered across Phoebe's face but did not linger. She opened her Valentino purse and began rifling around for something.

She knows where he is. She's just not saying. It was time for Alison to try on her acting shoes — Kelly and Christine did not corner the market on drama. She needed to guilt Aunt Phoebe into spilling it. "I just miss him so much," Alison wailed, forcing her voice to crack while she pulled a tissue out of her pocket. "It's terrible!" Alison sobbed and hid her face.

"Oh, Alison, I know you do." Phoebe set down her purse and moved closer to her niece. Alison knew her aunt loved playing the good mother hen. Aunt Phoebe put one arm around her while she fingered her pearls with the other hand. "I'm sure he's fine," she said unconvincingly.

Alison sobbed again.

"Honey, don't cry. We just need to get your mother through the trial," Phoebe said softly. "Then we'll worry about your father."

Lifting her head, Alison caught and held her aunt's gaze. She knew Aunt Phoebe could see her eyes were dry. Alison did not try to hide it. "You didn't answer the question," she said. "Can you help me contact my dad?"

"I don't know where he is," Phoebe said, letting her pearls slip out of her fingers and removing her arm from around Alison. "But you can always talk to me, or to your grandmother. And you know Kelly is always there for you, even though she has her mind on Chad right now, the poor thing. You've got plenty of family support."

Alison inched away from her aunt and stared out the window, saying nothing. The pearl-clutching toad had more Diamond in her than Alison had given her credit for. But Alison was a Diamond, too. And when Aunt Phoebe turned to stare out the window, Alison reached into her aunt's open purse and pulled out her BlackBerry, quickly slipping it into her own bag. If Aunt Phoebe would not tell her where her father was, she'd find out for herself.

Chapter Twenty-four

It looked good — really good. And the only way the belt in the window of Neiman's could possibly look any better was if it was slung around Kelly's hips. She squinted at it through her sunglasses and considered trying it on.

Still staring at the window, Kelly noticed something reflected in the glass — something even better than the glittering belt — cruising down the sidewalk behind her. *Now* that *is something worth trying on*, Kelly thought. And with one well-calculated missstep, she pulled off her sunglasses and backed into the handsome not-so-stranger, letting him break her fall.

"Oh!" Kelly cried. "I'm so sorry. I wasn't

watching where I was going!" She regained her balance but kept her eyes downcast, straightening her outfit. Then, when the moment was just right, she looked up into the smoky eyes of Dustin Simon.

"Oh," Kelly said again, like it was a surprise. "It's you."

"Kelly?" Dustin smiled easily, pushing his dark blond hair out of his face. His curls had an adorable way of flopping into one of his eyes. He looked a few weeks overdue for a trim, but it went great with his light stubble and "I couldn't care less" style.

"So, what are you doing here?" Dustin asked. "Taking a little break from the hospital?"

"Actually, I was just going to head over there," Kelly lied. "It's so depressing, though, don't you think? I don't mean Chad; I know he'll be okay. But all of those sick people. It's just so, I don't know, grim or something."

Dustin looked amused. "So Kelly Reeves isn't too crazy about sick people. . . ."

Kelly started to blush, then blushed harder when she felt her face growing warm. She couldn't remember the last time a guy had made her feel flustered — if one ever had. But she was pretty sure the wink Dustin added counted as flirtatious, so she took that as her cue to keep the conversation going.

"Hey, Dustin, as long as you're here, I'd *love* to get your opinion on something."

Dustin cocked his head. *Wow, he's cute.* Kelly bit her lip to remind herself to keep cool. "What do you think of that belt?" Kelly pointed to the jewel-encrusted sparkly number on the mannequin in the window.

Dustin squinted at it. "Are those diamonds?" he asked, stepping forward and pushing the floppy hair back again.

"No." Kelly laughed. "They're Swarovski crystals."

"Right." Dustin gave Kelly a superslow smile. "I think they're your color."

He was joking again, right? Kelly laughed harder.

"But, um, I gotta get going." He jerked his thumb in the direction he had been heading. "I've got some work to do."

"Right. Don't let me stop you." Kelly tried to keep the disappointment out of her voice. She hoped she didn't sound like a letdown kid. "They must give you tons of coursework in college." Then, standing on tiptoe, she kissed Dustin's bristly cheek. Kelly wasn't usually a big fan of unkempt guys, but somehow Dustin's stubble just made him more irresistible.

Dustin looked surprised by the kiss, but not in a bad way. He put his hand on the spot where Kelly's lips had touched his face and squinted at Kelly, like he was figuring her out. Kelly tried hard to keep her cheeks from turning red . . . again.

"Better go," he said slowly, finally looking away. "Gotta keep up with that, uh, coursework." He shook his head once, really slowly, like she was too much. "Later, Ms. Reeves," he said with that slightly amused smile still playing at the corners of his mouth.

As he walked away Kelly felt the same smile pull at the edges of her lips. *Later,* she promised herself.

Chapter Twenty-five

Tom pulled himself out of the heated pool and, ignoring the chill in the air, walked across the tile and through the glass doors into the main house. He was soaking the carpet, but he didn't care. He'd swum two miles and felt great. And there was nobody around to yell at him. He was gloriously alone. Dad was working, Deirdre was shopping, and poor Zoey had been taken along as a hostage.

Shaking like a dog, Tom sent water flying all over the front hall before pulling a towel over his shoulders and stooping to gather up the mail the postal carrier had pushed through the slot near the door.

Along with a heavy stack of Deirdre's fashion and gossip magazines and the usual bills, there was a plain manila envelope addressed to Tom.

His name was written across the front in blue ink, and the handwriting was familiar. But the address below it was penned in black and written in all caps. Tom turned it over, his wet hands smearing the ink. There was no return address, but there was a note on the back in the same blocky writing as the address.

TOM —
FOUND THIS AMONG AUDRA'S THINGS. YOUR NAME
WAS ON IT. THOUGHT YOU MIGHT LIKE TO HAVE IT.
DR. DOUGLAS C. WILSON

That was why the handwriting was familiar. The envelope was from Audra. She was the one who had written his name.

Suddenly Tom felt his skin turn to gooseflesh and he wished he had taken the time to dry off. Dropping the rest of the mail on the side table, he walked into the living room and sat down.

Tom's hands were shaking. He felt like he

was being watched, or haunted. He resisted the urge to run to the window and look for Audra's car across the street.

"She's stalking me from beyond the grave," he whispered to himself. It was supposed to be a joke, only it wasn't funny.

Slowly Tom ripped the seal on the manila envelope, allowing himself to hope for the first time that Audra had actually come through with the one thing she'd often promised but never delivered — his mother's psychiatric file. Carefully Tom reached in and pulled out a single Xeroxed piece of paper. Tom tipped the envelope upside down and shook it. There was nothing else.

Okay, so it's not the whole file, Tom said, looking closer and trying not to be disappointed. One side of the paper was covered in doodles and notes in the same block writing as the message on the outside. And at the top of the page, along with a date, was written PATIENT: SUSAN RAMIREZ.

With a gulp, Tom began to read the scraps of information littered across the page.

FEELS LIKE STUMBLING BLOCK IN D'S CAREER.

IN THE WAY. NOT SLEEPING. FEARS HUSBAND.

FEARS DIVORCE. WEAKNESS MAKES D ANGRY.

SOME DAYS S DOESN'T FEEL SHE CAN GO ON.

HAS TO FOR THE KIDS. WANTS TO PROTECT

THEM — BE THERE FOR CHILDREN.

And that was all.

Crumpling the page into a ball, Tom threw it across the room, wishing he could throw away his helpless feeling as easily. He felt mad — mad at Audra for not showing this to him earlier, and for only giving him one tiny piece of the huge puzzle. She had probably been planning to dole out scraps of information one at a time to keep Tom hungry — keep him asking for more, and dependent on her.

More than mad, Tom felt helpless that he had not been able to help his mom. The date on the paper was just weeks before she died. She had been scared! She knew she was in the way of Tom's dad's career. She knew she was in danger.

Slamming his fists down on his thighs, Tom stood up. He crossed the room quickly, swooped up the ball of paper, and smoothed it out. His mom had kept too much to herself, too many secrets — and look what had happened.

Tom would not make the same mistake.

Chapter Twenty-six

Kelly draped her pink rabbit-fur cropped jacket over the waiting arm of Grandmother Diamond's housekeeper, Louise, and stepped into the three-story foyer ahead of her father, Bill. She had been feeling pretty good since her encounter with Dustin the day before and was determined not to let this mandatory family brunch ruin her mood. It was not going to be easy. Aunt Helen's trial had everyone worked into a lather. Kelly's mother Phoebe was so over-wrought she'd blabbed about her missing BlackBerry the whole ride over — she just *knew* the prison guard had swiped it. Worse, Aunt Christine had just flown in for a visit — the first since Kelly had found out she was her *real* mother. Christine hadn't even bothered to call Kelly in advance to let her know she was coming. Kelly was not looking forward to the reunion.

Taking a deep breath and pasting on a wan smile, Kelly entered the dining room right on time. Francesca was ringing the bell and Grandmother had not yet arrived. Quickly Kelly surveyed the seating plan. In the Diamond family it was easy to find out your standing with Her Highness — just check your seating assignment.

Phoebe practically squealed as she read her place card to the left of the head of the table. She'd been promoted. Across from her, Alison was hovering, waiting to sit down in the seat of honor at Grandmother Diamond's right. The chair at the other end of the table, across from Her Highness, was hardly ever filled. Kelly wondered if it used to seat the grandfather she never knew — and nobody ever spoke of — or if it was once Aunt Helen's chair.

The seat of least favor, in the far left corner of the long rectangular table, had this morning been reserved for Aunt Christine — punishment for spilling the beans, no doubt. Kelly was glad to see her grandmother was still mad about that piece of news being broadcast. Directly across from her, Kelly's dad had a spot of little significance. Kelly was stuck between Alison and Christine.

Kelly rolled her eyes, uttered a terse hello to her least-favorite relatives, and sat down between them.

Almost showtime.

Phoebe did the honors, breaking the silence with requisite pleasantries. "How was your trip, Christine? Will you be staying long?"

Kelly took a small sip of her freshly squeezed orange juice and thought up a few questions of her own. *Is that a new nose? Are you sure you got the right size? Do you have any other children besides me?*

"Fine, thanks. Just a few days." Christine smiled. Her face barely moved.

Then the hard-hitter entered the field. Grandmother Diamond came into the room just as Francesca peeked in again from the kitchen where she had the hot food in a holding pattern.

While Bill scurried around to the head of the table and pulled out Tamara's chair, Phoebe leaned in and gave the air near her cheek a kiss. "You look lovely today, Mother," she cooed.

"How nice that we're all together." Grandmother Diamond handed over her cane and allowed her son-in-law to push in her throne.

Kelly smirked at her cousin, noting that "all" was a subjective word. Neither of Alison's parents were there. . . .

"Really, Mother, I'm never in town and when I am, you seat me in the corner!" Aunt Christine whined as Francesca brought out the platter of eggs Blackstone.

Bad move, Kelly thought. *Definite point deduction for that.*

"Stop whining, Christine. It is not a demotion. I simply thought you'd want to sit next to your *daughter*," Tamara said flatly. "You left so quickly after sharing the news, I do think Kelly missed you. I'm sure you two have a lot to talk about."

Two points for Her Highness.

Aunt Christine's coffee cup clattered onto her saucer. She glared accusingly at her sister. "You told her?"

Phoebe held her own. "I didn't say a thing," she fired back haughtily. "Unlike you, I can keep a secret."

Wow. Two points for Mom. Kelly felt almost proud. This was a definite improvement over Phoebe's usual simpering. Apparently sitting next to Tamara made her feel empowered.

"Kelly was the one who told me," Grandmother Diamond said. "And she had every right to." She stared evenly at Christine. "The only one out of line in this situation was you."

Beside Kelly, Aunt Christine stared daggers. Kelly turned and flashed her a dazzling smile — the one she had inherited from her. Aunt Christine could stare all she wanted. Wrapped in her grandmother's bulletproof armor, Kelly was safe.

Chapter Twenty-seven

It was at least seventy degrees in the dining room, but Alison felt chilled. She looked slowly from her grandmother to her cousin and back. Their eyes were locked. They were smiling at each other appreciatively, smugly. And it freaked Alison out.

When the brunch began, Alison was just grateful that the conversation had nothing to do with the trial. She was glad that the heat was all on Kelly and Aunt Christine. She was hoping for a chance to sit back and watch Kelly squirm. But Aunt Christine was doing the squirming and Kelly and Aunt Phoebe were coming out smelling like roses.

Alison shuddered. Grandmother Diamond and Kelly were a dangerous duo. And now that Aunt Phoebe was proving her own deceptive prowess . . . ugh.

The moment the last dish was cleared, Alison set her napkin on the table. "Grandmother, may I please be excused?" were the first words she had spoken at the meal. To her relief, her grandmother nodded her assent.

Pushing back her chair, Alison left the dining room and hurried upstairs to gather her stuff. She wanted to get to the hospital ASAP. Her visits always made her feel better.

Tossing her homework and a novel into her pink Dior bag, Alison dashed downstairs. She could hear the sound of her family still spitting verbal barbs at one another in the parlor over tea. How cozy. She hoped Kelly wouldn't notice her slipping out. The last thing she wanted was for her cousin to follow along on her visit.

Tapping her foot impatiently on the marble floor, she waited for Fernando to pull the car around. Where was he? The patterned toe of her Emilio Pucci slingback slipped on a bit of paper under the foyer table. It was the table where

Louise deposited Grandmother Diamond's mail. A large pile lay unsorted on the top — but under the table, right beside Alison's toe, was a picture of Belize.

It can't be, Alison thought. She quickly reached down and snatched the postcard up. She tucked it under her jacket and walked outside. She did not want to chance looking at the card until she was alone, because she was almost certain it was from her father. She had only gotten one other piece of mail from him since he'd disappeared, and from that it was clear that most of what he was sending had been intercepted before it reached her, and probably destroyed.

Safe inside the Rolls, she waited until Fernando was deep into a car karaoke version of an old Green Day song before she slipped out the postcard.

Dear Alison,
I am sorry that I left without saying good-bye,
but I wish you would forgive me and write
back. The situation was beyond my control. I
wish I could call. It would be so nice to hear

your voice. But as you know, we are not
allowed phone contact in rehab. Please write
me, sweetie, even just to let me know you
and your mother are okay. Sticking together
is key.
Love,
Dad

Alison cleared her throat and stuffed the postcard into her bag. Seeing her dad's familiar handwriting made her miss him like crazy. She wanted to ask him about the key. Had he meant anything by that last sentence? Was it a clue, or a coincidence? *Don't worry, Dad. I'll track you down. I'll unlock the secrets. . . .*

She peered into her purse. Lying next to the postcard was Aunt Phoebe's BlackBerry. She'd had it for almost twenty-four hours, but hadn't yet brought herself to search through it. It *had* to have the information she needed. But if it didn't, she'd be back at zero, and she didn't think she could handle losing this last hope.

The Rolls came to a stop and Alison realized they were already at the hospital. "I'll get my own door," she said. Snapping her purse shut, she climbed out of the car and closed the door. Fernando nodded, turned up the music, and drove off.

Inside, the hospital was unusually quiet. The waiting room was practically empty and the nurses were all standing around the nurses' station chatting. Alison waved to them casually and they waved back. She visited room 308 so often, she knew most of the day staff by name.

Outside Chad's room, Alison paused. She felt oddly nervous as she reached for the handle. She could hear a male voice inside. Her heart hammered. Was it Chad? Was he awake?

Slowly Alison opened the door a crack. The voice was not Chad's, but it was familiar. It was Tom. Alison smiled involuntarily. Tom was there already and talking to Chad.

Alison's smile faded when she heard what Tom was saying.

"I'm so sorry, Chad." Tom was choked up and talking softly. "I wish you could know how sorry I am about all of this. About Kelly. About everything."

It was too late to knock, Alison decided. She

ought to leave, but she could not tear herself away. At the mention of Kelly's name, Alison's heart lurched.

"You know how much I've always liked her," Tom went on. He sounded like he was crying a little. "I just wish . . ."

Alison wished she could turn back time. Why should it surprise her to know Tom was crazy about her cousin? Wasn't everyone?

Taking her shoulder off the door, Alison let it click shut. She did not want to hear any more and didn't mean to eavesdrop. She turned to leave — not sure where she was going — and almost ran into a nurse carrying a huge bouquet.

"Hey, you going in? You want to take these?" the scrub-clad woman asked. She was almost completely hidden behind the enormous, tropical flowers.

"Um, yeah," Alison said, accepting the giant arrangement. She glanced down at the tiny card stuck in the foliage.

Chad, May you have a whole new perspective when you wake up. Good luck, X

X? Alison reread the card. *X?* Since when did Chad know *her?* Alison felt an odd mix of jealousy and admiration. She'd had no idea that X was a Chad fan. It was so strange. Since Chad had fallen into a coma, she felt like she had learned more about him than she had when they were dating.

"Delivery," Alison called loudly as she pushed her way into the room. She flashed Tom a smile as she set the flowers down with the other bouquets on the window ledge. She was determined to ignore everything she had heard. But when she looked over at Tom, he looked even sadder than he had sounded. He *was* crying. Without thinking, or saying another word, Alison walked over and wrapped her arms around him.

Tom hugged her back, letting his head rest on hers and his damp tears fall into her hair.

As Alison leaned against him, she felt the warmth and comfort of his arms around her. This, she realized, was what she was here for. This was what she was missing and wanting . . . from Chad.

Chapter Twenty-eight

Tom squeezed Alison back, letting the tears come. He hadn't known it would feel so good and so terrible to cry. Nor had he known, until now, how it would feel to hold Alison. That was good and terrible, too.

"I'm sorry." Tom pulled away, wiping his face. He had not meant for anyone to see him that way, especially Alison. But Alison didn't look freaked at all. She looked at him with her sweet blue eyes and an expression that seemed to say, "I know."

"This morning it was all getting to me," Tom explained. "So, I was talking to Chad. . . ." Tom forced a laugh. He hoped he didn't sound like an idiot — spilling his guts to a guy who couldn't even hear him.

"I talk to him, too," Alison confided. "He's a good listener."

She was making this easy, Tom realized. Alison was a great listener, too — even better than Audra had been. Cuter, and a lot less freaky. "It's the guilt," he said. "I can't shake it. I feel like it's all my fault. The coma. Audra. All of it."

"There was nothing you could do," Alison said gently. "Chad is sick — not even *he* knew that. And Audra, well, she was sick, too."

Tom nodded. He supposed she was right. The file page he'd gotten in the mail was extra proof. Just talking about it, just having her listen, brought him relief. He'd never felt as safe with another person as he did with Alison right now.

Tom resisted the urge to sweep Alison up in another hug. Instead he sat down and turned back to Chad.

Alison sat quietly beside him. He felt her studying his expression and wondered if she could read his thoughts.

"You don't have to go through this alone,"

she said softly. "Your sister really cares about you. You shouldn't shut Zoey out."

Tom gulped. He didn't want to cry again. He looked into Alison's caring face. She was so right. And so beautiful . . .

Without thinking, Tom reached out and touched the soft skin on the back of Alison's hand. He ran his hand over hers, turning it palm up. Slowly their fingers intertwined.

Alison's eyes grew wider, but she did not pull away. Tom's heart thudded as he leaned closer — just as the door to room 308 swung open. Stafford's most frighteningly cool student stood in the doorway, smiling enigmatically.

Inhaling sharply, Tom dropped Alison's hand.

Chapter Twenty-nine

In about two seconds X digested the whole scene. Mr. Popular was still sound asleep in his coma cocoon. Ex-Best Friend was making a misty-eyed move on Ex-Girlfriend. (Funny how guilt and grief could bring two people together.) And the flowers she had sent were by far the best in the room. That was to be expected, of course. She was very well paid.

"Well, hello." X smiled as she breezed in. She walked straight up to Chad and laid a hand on his forehead. He looked so peaceful.

"What are you doing here?" Tom demanded.

X looked up. The Ex-Best appeared disgruntled. He was covering embarrassment with bravado. Boys. *Don't worry. I won't linger*, X thought, still smiling. *Just making the rounds.* "I was just visiting my great-aunt," X explained easily. "And I thought I'd stop in and see Chad. Coma patients respond well to visitors. Did you know they are often aware of *everything* that is going on around them?"

Ex-Girl looked nervous. X looked away and gazed down at Chad tenderly. Poor kid. Then looked back at his tortured Ex-Girlfriend. Poor kid.

It was as X suspected. Alison Rose really *was* all wrapped up in Chad. But now the silly thing was falling in love with Tom. That would certainly make things sticky.

"I think it's great you two are here. You must really care about Chad. And since there's no need for superfluous visitors..." X walked toward the door and nodded over her shoulder. "See you at school," she called.

The door clicked shut behind her and X pulled out her phone to make a report.

Chapter Thirty

Zoey walked down the hall to her room. DA Daddy and Deirdre were out with campaign donors for Sunday dinner, Tom was still at the hospital, and Zoey was all alone after a great afternoon with Jeremy. Just as soon as she ditched her bag she was planning a gourmet dinner of cheese puffs and Häagen-Dazs in front of some reality show theater. Magnifique. Opening the door to her room, Zoey flung her bag toward the bed without looking.

"Oof." The bag hit somebody.

"Aah!" Zoey screamed and flicked on the light, ready to run. Tom was seated on her bed, rubbing his stomach where her heavy books had landed. "What are you doing in here?" Zoey yelled. She hated being taken by surprise. And she was not crazy about the idea of her brother hanging out in her room without permission, either.

"Whoa." Tom put his hands up. "Don't shoot. Again. I come in peace."

Zoey quickly scanned her room. Nothing was disturbed. And it was too dark for Tom to have been looking at anything, anyway. Calming down a bit, Zoey took her hands off her hips. She knew her brother was not a snoop, and for that she was grateful. She had some pretty important secrets hidden in her room, like Alison's stolen file — the one that could hurt Tamara Diamond and help Helen Rose, if Alison came forward with it.

"Sorry." Zoey kicked off her shoes and reminded herself that Tom was coming around to her side these days. Finally. And if she didn't want to reverse the direction they were heading in, she'd better lighten up.

"I didn't mean to scare you. I, uh, have something . . ." Tom trailed off. Zoey noticed the funny look in his eyes and sat down on the edge of her bed, ready to listen to whatever Tom had to say. He was so serious, it was making her tense. He held up a sheet of paper.

For a second Zoey thought maybe Tom had found Alison's file after all. But the paper he put down on her bed was a single sheet — a printout of an Internet article.

Zoey glanced at the article and waited for an explanation. Tom pointed at the picture of a car being pulled from a lake.

The image made the hair on Zoey's neck stand up.

"It's about Mom," he said. He was waiting for her to see something, but Zoey had no idea what. She could feel him growing frustrated beside her, so she leaned in and studied the article closer, even though an article about her mom's death was the last thing she wanted to look at. It had all the facts that were now a part of Zoey's history: the date their mother died, where, when, how — just over four years ago, in Great Falls Lake, drowned in a car accident. This was nothing new.

"Look at the car," Tom said, his voice shaking.

Zoey looked at the pixelated picture. The car was a four-door sedan — a Mercedes. Her dad's Mercedes. "It's Dad's car," she said, confused.

"I always thought Mom crashed in her own car," Zoey said. "I guess we were too young and too upset to notice the details." She still was not sure what Tom was getting at.

"And that's what Dad wanted us to believe." Tom sounded sinister when he spoke.

"Hang on a second." Zoey stood back up. "Are you saying what I think you're saying? Are you saying Dad drove Mom into the lake?"

"All I'm saying is that she couldn't have driven herself in his car. And that when I confronted Dad about it at the wedding reception, he didn't deny what he'd done."

Zoey's mind reeled. She didn't know what to think. She stared at her twin, wanting him to take it all back. She was not sure she could even handle the idea that her dad was responsible for her mom's death. It was too horrible. Zoey started talking fast. "Maybe she got in the wrong car. She was out of her head, right? And if she couldn't shift, that might be why she drove off the road. I mean . . ." There had to be an explanation.

"But, Zo, she left from home. And Dad was supposedly at the office. Wouldn't his car have been there with him?" The calm in Tom's voice was starting to make Zoey's skin crawl.

"You're jumping to conclusions." Zoey could not believe what Tom wanted her to believe. "Things aren't always what they appear. Like how I didn't kill Audra. Dad wouldn't. He couldn't!" Zoey sat down on her bedroom floor. Her eyes welled with tears.

"Couldn't he?" Tom asked.

Chapter Thirty-one

Kelly ignored the chime of the grandfather clock in the hall outside her bedroom as she fixed an out-of-place lock of hair. It was nine-thirty. She had taken over an hour to choose today's outfit, and if rules still applied, she was already very late for school. Luckily they didn't. Stafford was still in recovery from the double tragedy, and she could always tell the teachers she'd had a counseling session. The endless supply of slack was the one thing she would miss when she dumped Chad for his older brother.

Ready at last, Kelly opened the front door and stepped outside. But instead of seeing her driver, Tonio, waiting for her in the family's black SUV, she saw the sporty Mercedes Aunt Christine kept in Silver Spring. And Aunt Christine was seated inside, beckoning.

"What?" Kelly asked, not moving from the porch. The two of them had not spoken since Sunday's prickly brunch.

"Get in," Christine said, patting the passenger seat. She had the top down, like she had forgotten she was in Silver Spring and not So Cal, and that it was forty-five degrees. "Your mother is going to testify today."

"You are?" Kelly could not hide her surprise.

Christine shot Kelly a nasty look. "The one who raised you," she snarled. "Just get in. I won't bite."

"Yeah, right," Kelly muttered, but she climbed into the shiny sports car. Whatever her motive, Aunt Christine's offer to take her to the trial sounded better than school. Luckily she was dressed for anything in Da-Nang embellished cargos and a skinny blazer.

The drive to the courthouse was quiet. Kelly was certain Aunt Christine had something to gain by bringing her there, but had no idea what it was. And she had no intention of giving her the satisfaction of asking. She would just have to stay sharp, ready for the trap.

The two blonds clicked into the courtroom just as Phoebe was being sworn in. As she watched her mother raise her hand and promise to tell the truth, the whole truth, and nothing but the truth, Kelly smirked. As if her mother could get away with anything else. Phoebe Reeves was a terrible liar.

Plunking down next to Christine on a hard bench at the back of the courtroom, Kelly prepared herself to be bored out of her mind. Her mother's testimony was sure to be as dull as dishwater. There was no way Phoebe would say anything too bad or too good about her sister in public — she was far too much of a wuss to risk crossing either Aunt Helen or Grandmother Diamond. And what could she possibly know about the details of the case? After checking out Aunt Helen (who looked pretty good for a jail-bird) and Grandmother Diamond (who looked as stiff and cold as an ice sculpture), Kelly settled in with her nail file for the long haul.

The prosecutor's first question made her head snap up.

"Mrs. Reeves, can you tell us about the conversation you and your older sister had on the afternoon of January thirteenth of this year?"

Phoebe cleared her throat. "I called Helen because I had some concerns about our accountant. He's okay, and local, but I was never very happy with the way he —"

"So you called to ask your sister for a recommendation," the prosecutor interrupted, putting Phoebe back on track.

"That's right." Kelly's mom nodded.

"And that's when Helen told you about her illegal tax shelter."

"Objection!" One of Helen's lawyers was on her feet. "Leading the witness."

Kelly dropped her nail file and leaned forward. This was fantastic!

The judge looked at the prosecuting attorney over the top of his reading glasses. "Sustained," he said.

"My apologies, your honor," the prosecutor said. He turned back to Phoebe. "And what did your sister tell you when you asked for a recommendation?" he asked.

Phoebe leaned closer to the microphone.

"She told me that taxes were for the poor and people who didn't know any better," she stated.

There was an audible gasp in the courtroom.

"Interesting," said the lawyer. "And then what did she say?"

"She told me that the trick was to get the cash out of the country before it was reported."

The gasp turned into a loud murmur, and the judge pounded his gavel to regain order. Kelly looked from Aunt Helen to Grandmother Diamond and back. Neither's posture or face showed any reaction.

The prosecutor turned to face the jury. "Before it was reported," he repeated. "And then what did she say?"

"Nothing," Phoebe said. "I did. I asked if she was worried about getting caught."

"And was she?"

Phoebe shrugged. "I don't know. She kind of dropped the subject, and then a few minutes later she told me she was so glad she had a sister like me — one she could trust to keep a secret." Phoebe paused, and Kelly sat straighter. She had a feeling something good was coming. "And then she said she'd be willing to pay for it."

"Pay for you to keep the secret?"

Phoebe nodded. "Yes."

"And did you accept her payment?" the prosecutor asked.

"Diamonds do not take charity or bribes," Phoebe said tersely. Kelly recognized Grandmother Diamond's words, and noticed her mother was looking right at her. Kelly thought she even saw Her Highness nod her approval.

Beside her, Christine snorted. "Don't they?" she mumbled under her breath. Kelly looked from her grandmother to her mother to her Aunt Christine. Only Tamara was smiling. As the prosecutor thanked her and returned to his seat, Phoebe had no expression. Christine was scowling. And even though all she could see of her Aunt Helen was her superstraight spine, Kelly was pretty sure that she was scowling, too.

As one of Aunt Helen's lawyers stood to begin the cross-examination, Kelly studied her mom. *She has more backbone than I realized*, she thought admiringly. *Either that or she has finally chosen the mightier of two evils*. Kelly had to admit she would rather have her grandmother in her corner than Aunt Helen. At least right now, when Aunt Helen's corner was ringed in bars.

"I think that's enough," Aunt Christine whispered. She got to her feet and left the courtroom, pulling Kelly along with her.

"Learn anything?" she asked as they clicked their way back to the car. Christine smiled at the people staring at them. Always the movie star.

"Trials aren't as boring as I thought?" Kelly joked. Actually, she was feeling pretty grateful to Aunt Christine for taking her to the show. Not only was it enlightening and entertaining, but it was going to kill Alison when she found out Kelly had gone when *she* couldn't. Kelly felt like she and Aunt Christine were on their way to being allies again.

She was wrong. Aunt Christine stopped in the center of the parking lot and whirled Kelly around by one shoulder. Her smile had disappeared and she spoke in a low, threatening voice. "No. I brought you because I want you to see how it is in our family — you stab my back, and I stab yours," she enunciated.

Then Christine's smile appeared again. But

it was not friendly in the least. Kelly had to work to remain expressionless.

"And," Christine went on, "I hope you appreciate just how much your little indiscretion with Mother cost me, and could cost you, too."

Kelly could not believe the words that were coming out of her aunt's mouth. Was that a *threat*? Over spilling one little secret? Aunt Christine was the biggest gossip in the family! She was the one who had told Kelly the secret in the first place! It wasn't Kelly's fault it had come back to bite her. The two were silent as they climbed into the car. Kelly crossed her arms over her chest. Her entertaining morning had taken a serious turn for the worse.

Aunt Christine put the keys in the ignition and started the car. Then she turned to Kelly and lowered her Chanel sunglasses. Her green eyes flashed. "You'd better learn where your bread is buttered, Kelly Reeves," she hissed. "You might be your grandmother's latest pet, but if you don't watch yourself, everything you own might just disappear."

Chapter Thirty-two

"Aunt Phoebe testified *against* my mother?" Alison blurted without thinking, staring down at the morning paper. Next to her, Grandmother Diamond was silently spooning up raspberries. Alison wished she could take her question back. She didn't really need an answer — it was right there in black and white.

"Yes, she did," her grandmother said coolly. "Your aunt Phoebe did what she had to. It seems your mother made some grave errors in judgment. I would not have expected that of her."

Alison was dumbstruck with a capital *D* for dumb. Of course Aunt Phoebe had testified against her mom. Phoebe did whatever Tamara told her to do. They *all* did whatever Grand-mother Diamond wanted, whatever it took to stay in her good graces. Even Alison.

Trying to look like she didn't care too much, Alison turned to the horoscopes. Her eyes scanned the words but she absorbed nothing. She was silently thanking her lucky stars that she did not have to testify.

Standing up before the judge, the jury, the cameras, and most of all her mother and grand-mother would be the worst thing imaginable. Alison did not want to have to choose sides in the Diamond/Rose war, in public or private.

She did not dare defy her grandmother — she was too powerful. Nor did she dare abandon her mother and give up any hope of being a family again. The trial was not going well for Helen, and the fact that Aunt Phoebe had tossed another log onto the fire burning at the base of Helen's stake gave Alison more sympathy for her mom. And gave her more guilt for having abandoned her mom to the fate Grandmother Diamond had designed for her by not coming forward with the documents she'd stolen. And a new fear was emerging in Alison now that things looked so dire: If her mother was convicted, would she have to go on living with her grandmother? For how long? She didn't want to think about it.

Standing up abruptly, Alison left her toast and scrambled eggs almost untouched. "I forgot I have to get to school early today," she lied.

"Go." Tamara waved her hand. "It will be nice to eat my breakfast in peace for a change."

Biting her tongue, Alison fled the dining room. Whatever. It wasn't enough that she had to act enormously grateful that her grandmother had taken her in — Tamara had to make her feel like a disturbance and a burden on top of it.

Alison needed to escape — ASAP.

Chapter Thirty-three

"Zoey!" Alison called. She'd been standing near the door of the lunchroom for what seemed like forever, waiting for her best friend.

"Where have you been?" Zoey asked, shooting a glare at one of the black armband mafia giving her the evil eye.

"Right here," Alison said. She grabbed Zoey's hand and pulled her toward the exit.

"I've been looking for you all morning," Zoey admitted as she followed Alison out the double doors and across the lawn to the gym. "You won't believe what Tom hit me with last night."

Alison couldn't imagine, unless he'd confessed his love for Kelly. That would go over *huge* with Zoey. "What?" she asked, trying not to sound impatient.

"He thinks Dad killed our mom."

Alison blinked. It took her a second to process the news. "He *what*?"

"I know." Zoey nodded. "He found this picture of Dad's car being pulled out of the lake. And Mom couldn't drive Dad's car."

"But that doesn't necessarily —"

"I know," Zoey said again. She was acting so cool about the whole thing, Alison couldn't believe it. "That's what I told him. But he's all fired up to go to the police."

Alison was quiet. Suddenly her family's secrets and lies and feuds seemed kind of . . . normal. "What'd you say?" Alison asked.

"I asked him to wait," Zoey explained. "Tom is so certain, but I'm just not convinced. I mean, I know my dad is slimy and all — he's a politician. But he loved Mom. I know he loved Mom." A funny look crossed Zoey's face. "Anyway, I think I got Tom to back down for a while."

"How?"

Zoey laughed drily. "I told him if we come forward now, Dad'll just bury it — he's too well connected. But if we wait until his campaign is in full swing . . ."

"Wow." Alison was impressed. She thought hers was the only family that had this kind of dirt on one another and used it in the most conniving way possible. "Remind me never to double-cross you."

"So what's going on with you?" Zoey asked as Alison led her around the corner of the gym, far from the parking lot or any windows. Nobody could see or overhear them, except maybe the chipmunks in the woods.

"Well, it's not quite that big. It's silly, really. I just didn't want to do this alone . . . in case it's nothing." Alison held up her aunt's BlackBerry. "Phoebe's," she said. "I took it."

"And . . ." Zoey was smiling. She liked it when Alison broke the rules.

"And I think my dad's rehab address might be in here. It's my only hope of contacting him. If this is a dead end . . . well, that's why I need you here."

"You got me." Zoey stood so her arm was pressing up against Alison's. Tentatively, Alison pushed a few buttons. She opened the address book and scrolled through names. When she got to the *R*s she felt Zoey grab on to her arm. Her old address was there, and her mother's jail address, and right after that was an entry for Jack Rose . . . in Belize! "There it is!" Alison breathed. She had her dad's address!

"So, what's that?" Zoey pointed at a number beside it.

"I'm not sure." Alison stared. "It doesn't look like a phone. Maybe a flight confirmation number." If so, it proved what Alison had only suspected before. Grandmother Diamond may have ordered it, but Aunt Phoebe was the one who'd done the dirty work of sending her dad away.

One question was answered. And now that Alison knew how to get in touch with her dad, she hoped he could answer a few more.

Zoey squeezed her hand. "So," she said. "What are you going to tell him?"

Chapter Thirty-four

Kelly sauntered out of Stafford Academy and stood on the curb in front of the marble steps, pouting and waiting for her ride. School had been a total yawn. The boys at Stafford were just that — boys. And Kelly was bored, bored, bored by them. It had been too long since she had seen Dustin, and she was thinking about what she should do about it when a rusted pickup stopped in front of her.

Tossing her shiny blond hair, Kelly stood on tiptoe to say something snarky to the incredibly rude driver for blocking her view with his mud-and-flaking-paint-covered monstrosity, not to mention parking in the spot where *her* driver stopped. But the cutting remark died in her throat when she saw the driver. It was just the person she wanted to see — Dustin!

"Hey, Reeves! Just the girl I was looking for," Dustin drawled.

"Really?" Kelly wished she had come up with something more original to say, but she was in shock. Her college hottie was right here in the flesh for all of Stafford to see. If only he wasn't driving a junk heap!

"Yeah, I, uh, lost my peachy ribbon." Dustin brushed his shirt where his apricot ribbon should have been. "Wondered if you knew where I could get a new one."

"You can have mine," Kelly offered. Careful not to snag her CeCe tie-front cashmere, Kelly unpinned the ribbon and slid into the passenger side of the truck, ignoring the junk on the floor. "Here," she said breathlessly as she leaned over and pinned it onto Dustin's plain black T-shirt. "Much better," she said, patting it and wishing she could come up with a reason to stay in his truck a bit longer.

"So, you wanna grab a coffee or something?" Dustin asked, looking down and making sure his pin was secure.

That was *exactly* what she wanted. "Let's go," she said, slamming the door. After texting Tonio that she didn't need a ride, she sat back against the torn upholstery. She could not have asked for a more perfect turn of events —well, except for the truck. In her mind, vintage was for couture, jewels, and maybe handbags. Maybe.

They pulled in to Hardwired and Kelly waited for Dustin to open her door. Wrong move. The guy was at the curb before Kelly let herself out. *So he'll need a little training after all,* Kelly noted. She wasn't put out — breaking him in would be half the fun. And at least he held open the door to the café.

"A skinny latte?" Dustin teased when she ordered. "Aren't you skinny enough?" Kelly laughed. He had a regular coffee and a slice of carrot cake. When the drinks were on the counter Kelly picked hers up and looked for a table for two.

"Oops. Forgot my wallet in the truck. Reeves,

you mind?" Dustin pointed at the amount due on the register.

"Sure." Kelly set down her latte and fished a few bills out of her burnt-orange bag while Dustin found seats by the fireplace. Normally she would be out the door before paying for a date. But Dustin's forgetfulness was part of his charm.

After she had paid up, Kelly slipped into the spot next to Dustin. "So, Dustin Simon," she said, flashing him her most flirtatious look. "Tell me everything."

What a day, Kelly sang to herself in her room. She could not get over her afternoon with Dustin. It had only been half an hour since he'd dropped her off, and for the past thirty minutes Kelly had been riding higher than high. Aunt Christine's threats were forgotten. Her mother's simpering . . . gone. Alison? Alison who? And Chad? He could sleep forever as far as Kelly was concerned.

The tone on her cell indicating she had a new text message brought Kelly back to earth. She flipped open the silver cell and read the screen. *What the . . . ?*

I'M BACK. HOPE U DIDN'T MISS ME. HAVE U BEEN GOOD? — TRUTHTELLER

Kelly stared at the phone, barely able to breathe. Truthteller? Kelly's old blackmailer? How could she be back? Wasn't she *dead*?

Chapter Thirty-five

"What should I say?" Alison asked, tapping her pen on her chin and looking over at Zoey sitting at the other end of the couch. Alison was taking a day off from the hospital and hanging out at Zoey's after school instead.

Zoey shrugged. "I dunno. It's not like I have a lot of experience writing letters to my dad. When I was away at boarding school I pretty much pretended I was an orphan."

Alison chuckled, then got serious. She had to get this letter to her father written and in the mail before she went home that night. And as usual, her grandmother expected her home for dinner at six-thirty.

Sighing, Alison leaned over the paper and began to write.

> *Dear Daddy,*
> *I got two of your postcards — I was so happy to hear from you! But it wasn't easy for me to find your address. Grandmother told me you went into rehab and thought it best we didn't communicate. I'm pretty sure she's been taking your letters. So please send stuff to Zoey's house: 462 Magnolia Court. Mom's trial isn't going well. If you'll just come home I know we'll be okay. So please hurry back. And Daddy, what is that key for??*
> *Love, Alison*

Alison was reading over the letter when Tom came through the front door. She quickly folded it and shoved it into the envelope that she'd already addressed.

"Hey," Tom greeted them as he headed straight for the kitchen.

"Hey," Zoey said.

"Hi," Alison added. She felt oddly shy as she

watched him get out a giant bowl and his trusty box of Cap'n Crunch.

It's so ironic, Alison thought as Tom poured milk onto his cereal. She and Tom had spent almost every afternoon together for the past two weeks, sharing their hopes and fears and vulnerabilities. But now that they were encountering each other in a normal place, Alison had trouble imagining even starting a conversation with him. What could she say?

"Hello?" Zoey interrupted her thoughts, shooting her a look. "Anyone home?"

Alison smiled at her friend, hoping Zoey hadn't noticed what she'd been staring at. She hadn't really explained to Zoey the bond she and Tom seemed to be forming, at least near Chad's bedside. "Speaking of . . ." She trailed off as she pushed herself up from the couch. "I'd better get this in the mail and get home before Her Highness decides I need a sunset curfew."

Zoey grimaced. "Right," she agreed. "I'll have to show you the *super* new outfit Deirdre got me some other time," she said, her voice dripping with sarcasm.

Alison laughed, slung her bag over her shoulder, and walked to the front door. She had to force herself not to look in the kitchen at Tom, who was crunching away. Whatever they shared only happened at the hospital.

Outside, the air was crisp. Alison buttoned her coat up to the top and shoved her hands into her pockets. After mailing the letter on the corner, she walked to the bus stop. Her grandmother would rupture a vein if she ever saw her on a city bus, but sometimes Alison liked to pretend she was like everyone else. By the time she got home it was just after six.

Alison stepped into the large brick mansion and paused for just a moment. The house was quiet. Breathing a small sigh of relief, Alison walked briskly toward the stairs. She didn't want to run into her grandmother — or Aunt Christine — before dinner.

Alison was just putting her foot on the bottom step when Christine's loud, screeching voice echoed through the grand foyer. "You are always looking for an excuse to punish me! Why don't you just admit she's still your favorite?"

Alison paused to listen, then tiptoed closer to the closed study door. Aunt Christine and her grandmother were having it out!

"I don't play favorites, Christine," Grandmother Diamond replied calmly. "I have done plenty for you — burying your mistakes, burning your little secrets. . . ."

Aunt Christine groaned. "Come on, Mother! Why do you constantly rub my nose in it? I am not the only Diamond daughter with a secret child. And at least I *acknowledge* mine."

Alison's eyes widened. Who was the other secret child? Her mind raced as she stood frozen outside the door. She was so engrossed in her thoughts and what she'd just heard that she didn't realize she was leaning closer and closer to a Chinese porcelain figurine on the table beside her. She knocked it over and it clattered onto the maple inlay.

Alison stared at the tiny statue for half a second to make sure it hadn't broken, then dashed up the stairs, leaving it lying on its side.

Inside the study, the voices were silenced.

Chapter Thirty-six

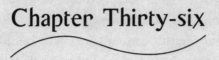

It was almost dark when Tom reached the cemetery. The sky was clouded and gray, and though it was still a little early in the year for snow, the air had that metallic smell that it always got before the first flakes fell.

Behind him, Tom heard the automatic window on Deirdre's car roll down. "You sure you don't want me to come along, sweetie?"

Tom shook his head without turning around. He was grateful for the ride — his stepmom would do anything to make him love her. But he definitely did not need her babbling in his ear right this second.

Though the cemetery was huge — the oldest

in Silver Spring — it didn't take Tom long to find Audra's grave. It was in the newer section, where the headstones had been laser-carved and occasionally had tacky color photos mounted on them. Thankfully, Audra's did not. It was a plain pink granite stone and read simply: AUDRA ARIEL WILSON, BELOVED DAUGHTER.

After Audra's funeral, Tom had skipped out on the burial. He just couldn't handle watching the coffin get lowered into the ground. But ever since he'd gotten that "letter" from her in the mail, he'd felt uneasy. He'd felt he needed to come here to say good-bye.

"So, I got your note, or whatever," Tom said out loud. "Thanks."

Wind rustled the turning leaves in the maple tree overhead, and Tom squeezed his eyes shut. Maybe he was the crazy one, talking to guys in comas and girls in coffins. But he went on.

"Thanks for listening, too. For being there. I bet you never thought you'd hear me say this, but I miss you." Tom took a deep breath, amazed to find he was actually feeling better.

"I guess what I really came to tell you is,

good-bye." He gulped. "Wherever you are, I hope you're happy now."

As if in answer, an icy gust blew a few fallen leaves onto the grave, covering the bare dirt.

"I'm not," Tom said softly, touching the cool stone of Audra's grave. "But I will be."

Chapter Thirty-seven

Alison walked into the dining room and sat down heavily in her seat at the table. The coma, the trial, her father . . . everything was taking its toll. She was tired and not the least bit interested in breakfast. But she had to show up at the breakfast table, just like she had to show up at school, and at family brunches, and at Tamara's beck and call.

Across from her, Aunt Christine spooned up a small bite of nonfat yogurt and fresh fruit. She was dressed in a tailored black suit and a white blouse, not at all her usual style. Christine was all about flash and color. There was nothing subtle about her. Usually.

Alison glanced at her grandmother's chair at the head of the table. It was empty, but Alison still felt Grandmother Diamond's presence. And she felt her aunt's eyes on her. Alison shifted uncomfortably in her seat and wondered if Christine knew she had overheard last night's argument.

"Are you going to court?" she asked abruptly, breaking the silence.

Christine nodded grimly. "I am. And so should you," she added pointedly. "The prosecution is about to rest."

"I can't." Alison raised her chin toward her grandmother's empty seat at the head of the table. She started to wonder where her grandmother was — then realized she really didn't care.

Aunt Christine set down her silver spoon, dabbed at her chin, and leveled her famous green eyes at her niece. "You can if you want to."

Chapter Thirty-eight

Kelly paced back and forth in her room. She was about to blow. Truthteller wanted another $500 — and had a new piece of information to make sure it was paid. Whoever TT was, she had seen Dustin and Kelly together. And now the snake was threatening to spread the rumor that Kelly was cheating on her comatose boyfriend with his older brother!

I wish, Kelly thought as she glared at the new text message on her phone. Landing Dustin would actually be worth 500 bucks. More, even. But she needed to do it her way. If she and Dustin were outed now by some amateur blackmailer it could seriously cut into her sympathy slack.

Kelly seethed as she counted out twenties and fifties and shoved them into a plain paper bag. It was a good thing she knew where her mother's cash stash was, or she'd have had to go to the ATM.

As she grabbed her cream-colored Prada peacoat off her chaise longue, Kelly wondered who TT could be. She hadn't seen anybody she recognized at Hardwired the other day — but she'd been so focused on Dustin, she wouldn't have noticed if Chad himself had walked in. And *anybody* could have seen Kelly climb into Dustin's truck in front of Stafford. The question was, who was dumb enough to be messing with Kelly this way? If her blackmailer wasn't Audra, what other psycho could it be?

Zoey Ramirez, Kelly thought suddenly. *She's definitely crazy, and she's definitely got a beef with me. Plus, she hangs out at Hardwired.* Kelly schemed as she left her bedroom, practically slamming the door. The murderess was asking for it this time.

"Bye!" Kelly shouted toward the kitchen, not waiting for a response as she headed out the door. Tonio was right outside looking bored and reading a car magazine, waiting to take her to school. "Change of plans," Kelly piped up from the back seat once the car was away from the house.

When her black SUV pulled up at the hospital, Kelly eyed the covered ashtray near the ambulance parking area — the assigned drop spot — like a hawk hoping to spot her new nemesis.

"I'll call for a pick up," she told Tonio as she jumped out of the car. It would not take long to drop the money, but she wanted to watch for Truthteller and see if Dustin happened to be inside. Maybe she'd actually get something *she* wanted out of this little expedition.

Kelly quickly walked to the ambulance area and dropped the bag behind the covered tray. Then she crossed to the main hospital entrance, went inside, and sat down to wait by the window on a chair completely hidden by a huge lobby plant.

Within five minutes Kelly was bored out of her mind. There were no cute paramedics to talk to, and the doctors and nurses all seemed to be in a hurry. She was just about to head upstairs to put in an appearance in Chad's room when a familiar voice caught her by surprise.

"Shouldn't you be upstairs?" Dustin asked.

Kelly's heart pounded and she got to her feet. "Shouldn't you?" she replied, beaming up at Chad's brother.

"I was just going there," Dustin said easily, offering his arm.

Kelly took it and tried to ignore the fluttery feeling in her stomach as she and Dustin walked over to the elevator. Before she knew it, the elevator doors were opening and they were getting out on the third floor.

Kelly slowed her pace just a little as they approached Chad's room, hoping Dustin would get the message. He seemed a little too eager to get to room 308, where her comatose boyfriend was lying in an adjustable bed with a plastic mattress. She didn't want to go in, didn't want to see him. Everything she wanted was right here . . . and it was time for her to take it.

"Dustin," Kelly said softly, tugging on his jacket sleeve. He paused slightly and she stepped in front of him and looked into his face, flashing her most dazzling smile. "Dustin," she murmured again, raising her hand to his shoulder. "You and I . . ."

Dustin narrowed his eyes slightly and nodded, as if he understood perfectly. His lips stretched into a slow smile.

Kelly tilted her head back slightly as everyone and everything around them faded. This was their moment — this was about the two of them. She could tell Dustin felt it, too.

She closed her eyes and waited. She heard Dustin's soft chuckle, felt him reach for her. Then Kelly felt him touch her cheek — and pinch it.

Kelly's eyes flew open. Wait, did Dustin just *pinch* her *cheek*?

"You're a cute kid, Kelly," Dustin said with a laugh. "Be good to my brother." He winked at her, then turned and disappeared in a cluster of medical staff.

Kelly stood stock-still in the hall wondering what had just happened. Dustin called her a kid! A *kid*??

Suddenly there was a commotion, and doctors and nurses started running into Chad's room. Through the open door Kelly could hear monitors beeping frantically.

"What's happening?" Kelly shrieked. Was Chad dying, or waking up? "What's happening?" Kelly shrieked again.

Nobody answered.

Chapter Thirty-nine

Alison felt like a criminal as she pulled her hat lower on her head and slipped into the courtroom, trying to look as invisible as she could. Finding a seat near the back, she sat down and tried to ignore the nervous kick in her stomach. She might feel better about being there if it hadn't been because of Christine. She'd taken her aunt's encouragement, but their whole conversation had left a bad taste in her mouth.

In the front of the courtroom her mother sat in a chocolate-brown suit and a light blue scarf that, even though she could not see them, Alison knew matched her eyes. Helen Rose's short hair was tucked under at the nape of her neck and her back was amazingly straight. Even after the second week of listening to her former allies and confidantes testify against her, Helen Rose was not broken; she was still Looking Good.

Alison resisted the urge to sprint to the front of the courtroom and show her mother that she was there. She'd missed most of the trial, but today she had made it. That counted for something, didn't it?

Alison tried to stay focused on the testimony, on the actual trial. But it was hard not to get lost in her own thoughts. It all went on and on. . . .

Alison scanned the crowd for familiar faces. She spotted her grandmother's white hair. Aunt Phoebe sat close beside her as usual. Christine was farther away. There were employees of her mother whom she recognized but did not know the names of. There were family "friends" and acquaintances. She even spotted X. And Jeremy, too. Some people just couldn't resist the spectacle.

Taking off her hat, Alison fanned herself with it. It felt hot in here, like there was no air. A couple of people stared at her, but she didn't care. The only person she really didn't want to see her was seated fourteen rows ahead of her and had not turned around all morning.

Maybe I should just go, Alison thought. She'd seen enough. And she could probably still get to the hospital before visiting hours were over.

Alison was just getting to her feet when she heard something that made her blood run cold: her own name. Her head jerked up as nearly everyone in the courtroom turned to stare at her, as if they'd known she was there all along. And then one of the lawyers repeated the phrase that was like a death knell:

"The prosecution calls Alison Rose."

Chapter Forty

Tom stepped into the elevator, relieved that he'd decided to cut class and come and visit Chad instead. He was still a little confused about the stuff that had happened with Alison, but that had nothing to do with his commitment to Chad. He would be there for him — forever.

As soon as the elevator doors opened on the third floor, Tom knew something was happening. The usually low-key wing was a flurry of activity. And the closer he got to Chad's room, the more his heart began to pound. The medical staff was all headed in the same direction. Something was going on with Chad!

Tom felt a moment of panic. What if Chad

was dead? Breaking into a run, Tom raced to room 308. A nurse tried to stop him at the door, but Tom ignored her. He forced his way past Kelly and inside. He had to get to his friend!

Please let him be alive! Tom thought desperately as he wove through the doctors and nurses crowded around Chad's bed. At last he saw Chad's face. His eyes were open! He was not only alive, he was awake!

"Chad!" Tom leaned over the bed and crushed his best friend in a hug, ignoring everyone and everything around them. "I am so sorry, man. I am so sorry." Tom could feel the wet tears running down his cheeks but he didn't care. It felt so good to finally be able to tell him — to have Chad hear and know. "You will always be my best friend," Tom sobbed. "You know that, right? Can you forgive me?"

Tom looked down at Chad's face and realized for the first time that it looked a little . . . blank. Chad blinked and stared up at him. Finally, his throat raspy and weak, he spoke.

"Who are you?"

Chapter Forty-one

Somehow Alison made her feet move. They steered her up to the front of the courtroom, to the witness stand where she would be judged by everyone present. She willed herself not to look at anyone — not her aunts, not her grandmother, and most of all not her mother.

As she pushed open the gate that separated the audience from the front of the courtroom, she wondered how the prosecution knew she was there. By the time she got to the stand she had figured out the answer: Aunt Christine. Christine had manipulated her, of course. She'd thrown Alison under the wheels of the Tamara

Train to get herself out. The words *You can if you want to* echoed in Alison's head.

Alison wanted to scream and pull out her hair. How could she have been so stupid? How many times had she suffered because she'd let her guard down with her family?

Countless times, she thought grimly as the bailiff asked her to place her hand on the Bible and swear to tell the truth.

Alison groaned inwardly. Which version of the truth did they want? Which version of the truth did *she* believe?

Alison repeated the oath, took a seat on the stand, and looked out. Time to face the music.

From her seat in the second row, Grandmother Diamond stared at Alison evenly. She did not appear surprised to see her. And there was something else in her gaze — a certain confidence, a certain smugness. It was as if she was daring Alison to tell everything she knew.

The papers Alison had stolen from her grandmother's vault proved that Tamara was also paying off many of Helen's key employees. The information was definitely material to the case. It could not only vindicate her mother, it could get her grandmother into serious trouble . . . assuming her grandmother hadn't already bought the judge, or the jury, or enough people who might otherwise come to her mother's defense. And assuming her mother was innocent.

Alison swallowed hard and looked over at her mother, who was staring at her with pleading eyes.

It had come to this. She was not surprised to see Alison on the stand, either. It was why she had been pushing her so hard to "be there for her." She must have known the prosecution was planning to call Alison as a witness. Her mother's reputation, empire, and freedom were on the line. Only Alison could help her now. Only Alison could save Helen Rose's life as she knew it.

Alison felt weak as the prosecutor looked at her with sympathy and prepared to ask his first question. She wished she had never found the papers, that she knew nothing about her grandmother's involvement in her mother's allegedly crooked business. She knew in her sinking heart that she was the only truly innocent Diamond in the room. Both her mother and her grandmother were guilty — of manipulating Alison mercilessly and using her as the rope in their game of tug-of-war. Finally they were both pulling so hard that this time Alison felt certain she would break.

Turning her head, Alison looked at her grandmother again. Suddenly she was certain of something else, too. This public "choosing of sides" was what Grandmother Diamond had had in mind all along. It was another masterful manipulation — one where the stakes involved her, her father, and her mother's freedom. Alison's leash had been yanked, hard.

Alison's hands shook in her lap. The time had come. After waffling since her mother's arrest, she would be forced to choose between two women who had jerked her back and forth between them since the moment she was born.

The federal prosecutor stepped up to the stand. "Alison Rose," he said gravely. "Do you have any evidence that could incriminate your mother in the matter before the court?"

The drama continues in
book five, *Nothing but the Truth*.
Here's a sneak peek.

With shaking hands, Alison turned on the
cold water and quickly splashed several hand-
fuls onto her face — a trick her mother had
taught her long ago.

*"You must always put the right face forward.
Never let people know what's really going on
inside."* Alison heard her mother's voice in her
head as she looked at herself in the mirror. Icy
droplets fell from her face into the basin, and
her blue eyes looked back, unsure.

I did it, and I survived, she thought, cupping
her hands for another splash. "It was the right
thing," she said aloud, trying to convince her
reflection. Guilt was seeping in and filling up

Alison's heart. But another, stronger emotion was there to push it out: relief. Her testimony was over, and she was still standing.

Taking a final deep breath, Alison shut off the water and ran her fingers through her shoulder-length, layered brown hair. She was preparing to go back to the courtroom when a stall door opened. X, a girl Alison barely knew from school, emerged wearing an apricot Tocca skirt suit with a white shirt and black tie. It was odd to see her out of the unusual school uniforms she wore to Stafford Academy every day. And it was disconcerting to see her here. The girl seemed to be everywhere.

X met Alison's gaze in the mirror and gave her a sad smile — a look that was sympathetic without being pitying. "Do you ever wonder if there really is a 'right' choice?" she asked quietly.

Alison stared back numbly.

"I mean, the truth can be so subjective," X went on as she washed and dried her hands. "It's really all about point of view. Don't you think?"

Alison tried to smile, as if being caught talking to herself in the bathroom after testifying against her mother was a silly lark. But her forced smile felt more like a grimace.

Suddenly an electronic ring echoed in the tiled room —Alison's phone. Heaving an inward sigh of relief at the interruption, she pulled the phone from her Bottega Veneta bag and glanced at the screen. *Tom Ramirez.*

"Excuse me," Alison said, slipping into the hall to take the call. Her heart was beating quickly. Tom never called her. It had to be about Chad.

"Hello?" she answered breathlessly.

"Alison? Alison, he's awake. Chad is awake!"

"Thank God," Alison said. Relief washed over her and all thoughts of the trial and X vanished. Chad had been in a coma for almost two weeks — the longest days of Alison's life. Finally, finally, Alison would get the chance to tell him that she loved him, too.

"How is he? Is he all right?" Alison asked as she clicked down the marble-floored hall. She was tempted to slip off her heels so she could run — she had to get to the hospital *now* — but there were too many photographers around. She picked up the pace as best she could.

"Tom, how is he?" she repeated.

Tom was silent for a moment longer. When he finally spoke, Alison's heart dropped.

"How soon can you get here?" Tom asked. "Something's wrong."

To Do List: Read all the Point books!

By Aimee Friedman

- ❏ South Beach
- ❏ French Kiss
- ❏ Hollywood Hills
- ❏ The Year My Sister Got Lucky

- ❏ Oh Baby!
  By Randi Reisfeld and H.B. Gilmour

- ❏ Hotlanta
  By Denene Millner and Mitzi Miller

By Hailey Abbott

- ❏ Summer Boys
- ❏ Next Summer: A Summer Boys Novel
- ❏ After Summer: A Summer Boys Novel
- ❏ Last Summer: A Summer Boys Novel

By Claudia Gabel

- ❏ In or Out
- ❏ Loves Me, Loves Me Not: An In or Out Novel
- ❏ Sweet and Vicious: An In or Out Novel

By Nina Malkin

- ❏ 6X: The Uncensored Confessions
- ❏ 6X: Loud, Fast, & Out of Control
- ❏ Orange Is the New Pink

By Jeanine Le Ny

- ❏ Once Upon a Prom: Date
- ❏ Once Upon a Prom: Dress
- ❏ Once Upon a Prom: Dream